A Daemon's Alliance

A DAEMONS & LUMENS NOVELLA

S. D. PAINE

"Never trust your fears, they don't know your strength."
-athena singh

To the dirty little readers who want to be chased…is your
heart beating faster?
Run.

AUTHOR NOTE

This book contains dark themes and the characters make questionable decisions. Tropes and triggers include graphic violence, rape/sexual assault (on page), torture, bdsm-related scenes, and explicit intimate scenes. If you need more information about the trigger warnings, contact me at sdpaineauthor@gmail.com.

For more information about this book and future books in the series, visit my website and sign up for my newsletter! www.sdpaineauthor.com

NOVELLA PLAYLIST

Find me on Spotify to listen to this Daemons & Lumens Playlist!

Warrior by Stitched Up Heart

Run Towards The Monster by Transviolet

Lonely Ever After by DAVVN

Love Story by Sarah Cothran

Dance You Outta My Head by Cat Janice

Lose Control by MEDUZA, Becky Hill, and Goodboys

Lose Your Breath by Anitta

Angel by Toby Mai

Predator by Yonaka

Tennis Court by Lorde & Flume

Him & I by G-Eazy and Halsey

Killer Queen by Mad Tsai

STRUT by EMELINE

Dead To Me by Chloe Adams

I Did Something Bad by Taylor Swift

Where Have You Been by Rihanna

The Nights by Avicii

Clarity by Zedd and Foxes

I Love It by Icona Pop and Charli XCX

Dark Doo Wop by MS MR

A Toast to the Ghost by Diggy Graves

Silence (feat. Sara McLachlan) by Delerium and DJ Tiesto

Monsters by Ariel Bellvalaire

Slave by Ramsey

Too Sweet by Hozier
Slow It Down by Benson Boone
Don't Go Insane by DPR IAN
After Dark by Mr. Kitty
Ritual by Bambie Thug

THE V.I.P. LIST

Aurora Valdis Bronwen - Mother of Lailah, Seraphina, and Michaela, murdered by The Obscuritas

Joseph Bronwen - Husband of Aurora, Father of Lailah, Seraphina, and Michaela

Lailah Valdis Bronwen - Oldest daughter of Aurora Valdis, murdered by The Obscuritas

Seraphina Valdis Bronwen - Middle daughter of Aurora Valdis

Michaela Valdis Bronwen - Youngest daughter of Aurora and Joseph

Tabitha "Tibby" Marsden - Tech wizard and friend of Seraphina, allegiance unknown

King Corson Ormaenus - King of Caligo and all daemons

Prince Belial Ormaenus - Oldest son, Prince of Caligo and loyal to the king

Prince Morax "Mor" Ormaenus - Middle son, Prince of Caligo

Prince Phenex "Phen" Ormaenus - Youngest son, Prince of Caligo

Andras Blackbyrn - Prince of The Obscuritas, son of Laszlo

Typhon "Ty" Radnor - Prince of The Obscuritas, son of Darren

Leviathan "Levi" Delano - Prince of The Obscuritas, son of Samuel

Devon "Dev" Parrish - Prince of The Obscuritas, son of Ezekiel

Laszlo Blackbyrn - King of The Obscuritas, Leader

Darren Radnor - King of The Obscuritas, Enforcer

Samuel Delano - King of The Obscuritas, Seducer

Ezekiel Parrish - King of The Obscuritas, Technician, Deceased

PAWNS & PLAYERS

Gremory Carrevaux - Daemon, General of the Royal Armies of Caligo

Ouriel - Lumen, loyal to Belial

Professor Lehmann - Obscuritas member

Audrey Kingston - Student at Law School, attends classes with Seraphina

Mr. Kingston - Father of Audrey Kingston, potential Obscuritas member

Arthur Nelson - Stepfather of Tabitha Marsden

The Malefica - Akin to witches, royalty in Tellisa

Mal-Regia - Royalty of The Malefica

IMPORTANT PLACES

Vespertine Hall - Estate located just outside the city of Boston, owned by The Obscuritas

The Cabin - Michaela and Joseph's current residence

Blackbyrn Manor - Estate located near Asheville, North Carolina, owned by The Obscuritas

Stella Terra (Stel-uh Tare-uh) - Planet of the daemons and lumens

Tellisa (Teh-lee-sah) - Country of the daemons and lumens

Caligo (Cal-ee-go) - Capital city of the daemons

Caelum (Kay-lum) - Capital city of the lumens

WORDS & PHRASES

The Obcuritas - Exclusive cult seeking otherworldly power

Umbra Noctis - Shadows of Night, secret sect of The Obscuritas

created by the Princes

daemons - monstrous creatures of myths and legends, varying degrees of magic/power relating to the elements

lumens - ethereal creatures of myths and legends, varying degrees of magic/power relating to the elements

stellatium (stuh-lay-tea-um) - a rare metal created from a dying star, powerful enough to kill a daemon or lumen

luxenite (lux-eh-night) - rare stone, magically charged to harness the power of a lumen's essence

tenebrite (teh-neh-bright) - rare stone, magically charged to harness the power of a daemon's essence

vis-el (veez-elle) - elemental power of the daemons and lumens, different from the spells wielded by The Malefica

mae domina - my lady/master

PROLOGUE

Tibby

My fingers flew across the keys, searching for data to back up the intel I just received. My stepfather was in the United States. Sweat coated the back of my neck, and I wanted to vomit. I hated that he still had such a visceral effect on me. And I hated that he was still alive. How the fuck he got all the way to this country without my knowing about it pissed me off.

I was more than just a hacker. My coding skills and ability to dig behind firewalls and anything else the tech gurus could conjure up were second to none. I wasn't cocky about much, but this was my domain. Someone managed to hide my stepfather's movements for two whole weeks, and now he was here. After seeing his name on a list of Obscuritas members, I started paying closer attention. He woke up from the stupid coma, and then he disappeared.

He landed in Salem two days ago. He was staying at an Airbnb close to some of the witchy landmarks the town was famous for. He was so close. Too close. I itched to call Seraphina and tell her, but for some reason, I paused. She was with *them*. The Princes. She was always with them. They did kidnap her, so it wasn't like she went totally willingly. I was trying—and failing—not to be jealous.

This was part of the plan, though, even if it happened in a slightly different manner than we originally planned. She had to get close to them. And it wasn't the first time she had slept with a mark either. Sometimes we had to do gross things to get what we needed. But this felt different. When I listened in on Dev eating her pussy like it was the most decadent dessert he had ever had, and she had a real fucking orgasm, I knew things were different. Just thinking about it made me horny all over again. And I definitely wasn't going to admit how many times I listened to that audio. I was so fucked up.

Voyeurism was obviously a kink for me, but telling Seraphina I fucked my own hand while listening to her moan for an Obscuritas Prince was out of the question. I should tell someone, though, maybe a therapist.

There wasn't time for therapy. Not when we were in deep cover and now my stupid stepfather was here distracting me. I glanced at the half-packed duffle bag sitting on my bed. When my facial recognition software alerted me that he was here, I started packing immediately. There were two small blades, a gun with a silencer, and a high-voltage taser next to the duffle bag. My fingers paused on the keys as I stared at the weapons. Could I do this? Could I sneak up on him and end his life on my own?

I could. I deserved this. And he deserved a nasty death for the abuse against me and my mother. My mother was only seventeen when she had me. Her parents kicked her out for being a whore. She was lost and alone on the streets with a newborn. My stepfather, Arthur Nelson, found us at a fast food place. He bought her food and said nice things. I wish I could be mad at her for it.

My stepfather liked teens, and she was too easy for him to pluck off the streets. He fed us, clothed us, even got a nanny to take care of me. But that was mostly for his benefit, so my mother was free of me and useful to him.

Until I was about seven years old, I thought my life was okay. I loved my nanny, and while my mother was not around often, she tried to look happy when she was with me. But on one of the days when she was gone, my curious mind finally got me into trouble, the kind no one recovered from. When a person witnesses something so horrible, the dark thoughts never go away.

My stepfather wanted people to watch what he did to the girls he caught in his web of depravity. I figured this out while playing with toys in my room. I heard sounds coming from my closet. When I slipped inside, I found a little peephole carved out with a window. On the other side, I saw a room I'd never been in before. My stepfather was there with a girl, and it was not my mother. She was gagged and tied to a bed, and he was touching her, doing things to her I didn't fully understand.

I started watching him through that peephole almost every night. I didn't realize until years later that he obviously planned for that to happen. I couldn't help the reaction I had to it, and I hated thinking about my stepfather every time it happened. Now, I had a love-hate relationship with my desire to watch others.

A half empty bottle of bourbon sat next to my computer, and I took a long swig. *Yeah. He had to die.*

Before I could think about it too much, I was racing down the highway in an unmarked car toward his Airbnb. It was about 2 a.m. now, very little traffic and even less light under the cloudy, moonless sky. I parked the car several houses down. I wore all black clothing and comfortable combat boots with little knives hidden on the sides. My white-blonde hair was covered under a dark-brown wig. My natural hair was short, a choppy pixie cut. I kept it this way because I liked wearing wigs and pretending to be someone else. Tonight I was just going for "inconspicuous cat burglar."

I stalked closer to the small house and picked the lock at the back door. There were cameras, but of course I had disabled them already. I loved the smart homes with all the digital tech. It was almost too easy to hack.

I studied the blueprint before coming, so even in the dark I knew where to go. The master bedroom was closer to the front, adjacent to the living area. The newer floors didn't creak beneath my light steps, and it was easy enough to move down the hall without making a sound. I quietly pulled the gun from my bag. When I stepped into the room, he snored loudly and rolled over. The blankets were thrown back enough to reveal his toned chest. My stepfather always slept in the nude. He wasn't ugly, which was probably why he lured so many women in so easily. His tanned chest rose and fell slowly as he slept. His brown hair was mussed, and his eyes fluttered while he dreamt. I wasn't sure how long I stared at him. Too long.

I stalked closer to the bed and slowly pulled down the blankets to reveal his naked body. I pointed the gun at his soft dick. I hated it. Hated that I knew what it looked like too intimately. I pulled the trigger, and the gun fired, barely making a sound, but the mess was instant. Blood squirted everywhere, and his dick was shredded by the bullet. He screamed so loud I jumped back. His eyes were wide and full of pain. Our gazes locked. Recognition and rage filled his dark eyes before he doubled over, cupping his bloody, ruined dick. I raised the gun again.

"I'm glad you're awake. I wanted you to know it was me." My voice shook with emotion, and he looked up at me with a snarl on his face. But I wasn't afraid. I pulled the trigger and the bullet went through his skull, blood splattering on the wall and all over the bed once more.

It was finally over.

"Well," a voice drawled from behind me, and I whipped around. "That was entertaining. You're going to be very useful to me, Tabitha."

Laszlo Blackbyrn's lips turned up into a cruel smile.

CHAPTER ONE

Michaela

For nearly a decade, I had been my father's good little girl. Well, sort of.

Father was all mixed up with evil men, and I couldn't sit still and do nothing while he played right into their hands. We'd end up as sacrifices, just like my mother, Aurora, and eldest sister, Lailah. Or crazy, like my second-oldest sister, Seraphina. And I refused to let either of those be my fate.

So I stole the book from his safe. I mean, I always put it back, so it was really just borrowing. He thought I didn't know the codes. He thought I didn't know anything, actually. It might have taken me a few years, but now I knew everything there was to know about this shit-tsunami of a situation that was my life. I might not have been some badass assassin like Seraphina allegedly was, but I was *not* helpless. I could do this. I would do this. I had stolen this book a hundred times now. Each time, memorizing a little more of the ritual I had decided on. The book was actually my mother's. Or it was her lover's. I didn't really know. My father didn't like to talk about the details. What I knew now was that this magic shit was real. Like really real.

At first, my father refused to speak about our family. He told me my mother and sisters had to go away. And he held onto that story so tightly, until I was finally mature enough and brave enough to ask him if my nightmares were real. I forced him to say the words out loud. My mother was dead. My sister, my strong and beautiful sister, Lailah, was dead. Murdered. I was thirteen years old and much too young for heavy shit like that, but he told me the truth, as much of the truth as he could. And then, over the last six years, I persuaded him to tell me more. I needed to know, was obsessed with it, really. And ho-ly shit, was my mind blown. *Daemons and lumens and cults, oh my!* They were real. My mother and Lailah were lumens. I should've known. Or maybe I did but refused to give my suspicions a voice until it was too late.

A memory of our family vacationing on the East Coast flashed through my mind.

Seraphina was pouting, sitting on the beach with her nose in a book. She acted like she wasn't impressed with the ocean. But I knew she was secretly afraid of it. Too many unknowns. I, however, relished the adrenaline as I dove into the waves. Lailah was with me, splashing and laughing as we swam. Mother called to us from the sandy shore, and we paused, treading water a few yards out.

I turned to Lailah and gasped, the playful words I was about to say stuck in my throat. She looked unimaginably sad. I was only ten at the time, but I knew my sister and could sense the heaviness of the moment.

"Why are you so sad, Lailah?" I asked, squeezing her arm.

Lailah stared out at the endless sea and sighed. "Just missing someone. A friend. The ocean reminds me of her. It was her favorite."

"Where is she?" My legs floated up, and I stared at the sky. "She should come here."

My sister sighed. "I wish she could."

Suddenly, our mother's terrified voice called out across the water. We turned to see a massive rogue wave rushing toward us. There was no time to swim out of its path; we were too far from shore.

I screamed, choking on salt water.

Lailah grabbed my hand. "Don't let go. Hold your breath. Now!"

I closed my eyes and sucked in a deep breath. Lailah shouted words I didn't understand, and suddenly we were rushing to the shore, as if we were riding the wave itself. In seconds, we landed in shallow water, our mother and father rushing toward us. I coughed up saltwater as Father lifted me into his arms.

"What happened?" My voice was hoarse and scratchy.

"Got caught in a big wave, sweet daughter. Are you alright?" Father brushed away the golden hairs sticking to my cheeks.

I nodded. "I think so." I turned to my sister, but she was farther off, speaking quietly with our mother.

Lailah's skin was glowing in the sunlight, she looked angelic, almost inhuman. Mother placed her palm on Lailah's cheek, and the glow faded. I saw Seraphina standing away from us, taking it all in with a shrewdness beyond her adolescent age. Her brow was scrunched as her eyes darted between Lailah and the ocean.

I tried to ask Lailah about it later that night, but all she would say was, "We were lucky."

It was the last trip we took as a family, and I never asked about it again.

Lumens were similar to what religious people called angels, in the sense of their ethereal beauty and god-like powers. But they were *not* all nice. Just like all daemons weren't evil. The

daemons, apparently, often had wings and horns and tails, which I was super curious about. My father was just an old-fashioned, Earth-bred human. Which meant I was a hybrid, half lumen, half human. And unfortunately, I had no power or magic. At least none that I could really access.

One of the many bits of information I pulled out of Joseph Bronwen over the years was that our mother told him she had our powers locked away for safekeeping, but Lailah's were harder to suppress because she grew up using them so often. The memory of how she saved us from that wave made more sense now that I knew what we were. Mother told our father my abilities would emerge when it was time. She should've known I wouldn't wait for whatever that "right time" was. And now I was more than ready to force the issue.

The stupid cult leaders of The Obscuritas were on our asses. My father was the worst at hiding. He was a good man with a good heart, which was why I thought my mother was drawn to him, but he wasn't cut out for this world of magic and mayhem. He refused to talk about Seraphina, so her lineage was more of a mystery. I think he hated himself for leaving her, but my mother told him it was part of "The Plan."

I had a love-hate relationship with "The Plan." Mainly because my mother wasn't here to answer all my questions. We just had to trust her. And I did trust her. Even though my heart was bruised and weary, I trusted her. But my father… his heart was half gone, and I didn't think he'd ever be whole again. So it was up to me to keep us safe and make sure those pricks leading that stupid cult didn't find us.

The book I "borrowed" from the safe was called *Rituum*

Lucis et Obscurum. It contained information about daemons and lumens. How to awaken powers, how to summon creatures, and many things I didn't understand. The text was in a language very similar to Latin. Learning Latin was a pain in the ass, but I was trying. The internet was basically my one and only friend.

I shivered as my fingers brushed against the cover of the ancient tome once more. It was made of flesh, but definitely *not* human. The skin glistened like it was infused with crystals and sent sparks of electricity into my veins. I felt connected to it, like the book recognized me somehow. The feeling reminded me of my mother. I had very few memories of her. But one of my first memories, from when I was very young, was of her touching my cheek and the same feeling rushing through my body. I could feel myself glowing under that touch. She smiled a sad smile before saying a mix of words I couldn't understand. And then it was gone. I never felt that rush again, until the first time I held this book. Sometimes I would take the book from the safe just to hold it and think of her.

But tonight, I was finally going to use the damn thing. The spell—at least that's what I was calling it—would *"summon a daemon to my aid."* There was another to summon a lumen, but for whatever reason, I felt called to the daemon magic. And besides, daemons were always portrayed in stories as scary, powerful beings. And that's exactly what I needed. Someone bigger and scarier than the men my father cowered to. It was only a matter of time until they came for us. And when they did, I would have a daemon at my side.

CHAPTER TWO

Morax

I paced the forest surrounding the royal castle, waiting for what was to come. I knew it would happen tonight. The hybrid would summon me, and I would finally be able to play a part in my father's demise. Phenex told me it would be soon. He was following the other one, the assassin. She was absolutely insane, so I was all too happy to work with the half-lumen girl instead. We'd been tracking the females since our brother, Belial, sided with our psychotic father and his plans of destruction. Phen and I knew from childhood our brother was rotting with evil. And while Father was terrible, Belial would be even worse. Phen and I had our own brand of darkness, but the endless abyss of cruelty Belial and our father craved was not it. When the prophecy was revealed, we knew the beginning of the end was upon us. And only with the help of Aurora Valdis's offspring could we stop our father and Belial from destroying us all. Gods knew I was ready to jump into this fight.

I slammed my fist into a tree, satisfied when it cracked and splintered beneath my knuckles. *What was taking the girl so damn long?*

I couldn't go to her on my own. I needed her to summon me. Our father had grown paranoid in his old age, and now all borders between worlds were guarded. We couldn't get to

Earth without the summons, though, not even he could do so. Aurora Valdis saw to that when she sacrificed herself some eight years ago. She and her lumen daughter perished, all access to the humans was cut off, and all daemons and lumens on Earth were essentially trapped. Belial and my father raged at her defiance. Phen and I were impressed. Although not surprised, knowing what we did of the prophecy. It was easier for Phen to accept lumens containing such power. I had always found daemons to be the superior race. Phen and his chaotic curiosity accepted change more easily than me.

And yet here I was, stomping around, listening for the words I knew the hybrid would say. My skin tingled with anticipation, and the power in my veins rushed to the surface, needing to be unleashed. But not yet, I couldn't risk Belial or one of his loyal followers catching me now.

The gentlest push of her magic brushed up against my own, and I paused. Any daemon strong enough to feel it could answer her call, but I was ready for it. This summons was mine. Her voice became clearer, uncertain, but strong, and it called to my soul. *How strange.* This feeling was different from the average summons. My blood began to sing, to crave more of her power mingling with my own. As she continued to say the words, the ritual grew in strength, and I said the words needed to accept her summons. My body turned to stardust, and I plunged through the abyss between worlds. To the human eye, I was a falling star; a beam of light flitting across the sky only long enough to make a wish. But only one little hybrid would be granted a wish from me today. I dropped to the earth, my clawed feet digging into the soft grass. I chose to stay in my natural daemon form for our first encounter. This little hybrid needed to see exactly what she brought into this world.

The air was hot and sticky here. I surveyed her world, noting the circle of salt and nearly spent candles surrounding me. I smirked. Salt would not hold a daemon captive. I stood tall, seven feet of muscle and daemon power. I surveyed the little lumen hybrid who called me here. She was quite beautiful. Her strawberry-blonde hair hung in messy waves down her back. Her frame was petite and thin, like a doll, so very breakable. I licked my lips, taking in the way her silky blue dress hugged her delicate curves. Her strange bright eyes, round with wonder, stared up at me without blinking, as if I were a mirage that would disappear if she looked away even for a moment. One of her eyes was the brightest blue, and the other was the color of cognac. Both eyes studied me with quiet determination. She was scared, but fierce.

The little lumen would not back down easily. I rather liked it. I grinned, giving her a look at my sharpened canines. She shivered, and my nostrils flared as I inhaled her strange scent. *No.* This was impossible. It was not to be. I didn't want it. I stepped back, stumbling out of the circle.

"How can you escape my circle so easily?" Her voice called to my soul instantly. My blood began to sing with desire to claim her. The voice of a weak, hybrid girl.

The voice of my mate.

CHAPTER THREE
Michaela

The daemon was freaking huge, easily over seven feet tall. And he looked exactly like a daemon from a damn romance novel. His skin was tinted red, but not bloodred, more like a sunset. His feet were clawed, like his hands. I could only imagine what damage he could do with those ridiculously sharp-looking talons. The horns protruding from his black hair spiraled out and looked equally dangerous. The wings at his back were jet black and feathered. I had the urge to reach out and stroke them. His eyes were a shocking gold, and I couldn't look away as he stumbled out of my protective circle.

His movements shocked me more than his appearance. Was that strange? Probably. I cleared my throat and tried to sound stronger than I felt. "Daemon, I have summoned you to my aid. You will obey me, following only my commands."

The daemon chuckled, and the sound sent a zip of desire straight through me. *Shit.* "What is your name, little girl?"

I grimaced and crossed my arms. My neck was getting seriously tired of staring up at him. "I am *not* a little girl. I am almost twenty years old and perfectly capable of defending myself."

The daemon bowed, and his eyes sparkled with delight.

Was he mocking me? "I am sure you are, but I am no mortal. If I wanted to break your sweet little bones, I could have done so already. And there is nothing you could do to stop me."

"But I summoned *you.*" I balled my hands into fists and inched my fingers toward the slit in my dress. There was a knife strapped to my thigh, and I was prepared to use it if I had to. I might have been small, but self-defense classes had taught me a few things. "You're *mine* to control. If you aren't going to submit, I'll summon another daemon who will."

The daemon growled and charged at me like something out of a nightmare. I whipped out my knife and thrust it toward him, ready to defend myself. He moved so fast, his thick, muscular neck suddenly pressed against the tip of my blade. "You won't be summoning any other daemons. Not. One. They cannot do what I can."

I stared into his golden eyes as his form shimmered. My body was rigid as I watched him shift before me. The claws retracted, the horns and wings slipped away, and before me stood a beautiful as hell man. He looked almost human— almost. He was easily a foot taller than me, even in human form, and I was 5'5". His muscles bulged as his captivating eyes stared down his aquiline nose at me. They were more muted now, hazel with flecks of gold. My knife remained pressed to his throat. My arm was beginning to ache from holding it up and out for so long. He grabbed my wrist before I could pull away, and I felt that rush of electricity again. I shivered, and his pupils dilated, taking me in.

"How did you get out of my circle?" I blurted out the words and then internally rolled my eyes.

He smirked down at me. "Salt does not keep a daemon locked up. You need ash. *Spodium.*"

A laugh burst from my lips, and my cheeks burned. "Oops. I thought it said sodium. Salt."

The daemon grinned at me, showing his fangs again. I think he wanted to laugh but held it back. I tried and failed not to stare at his sensual mouth.

"What is your name, feisty girl?" he demanded, his voice deep and commanding all of my attention.

The sound made my legs feel weak, but I refused to cower in fear—or the other thing I was definitely not feeling. I lifted my chin and stared into his god-like face. "My name is Michaela Bronwen. You can call me Michaela. Or master. Whichever you prefer."

The daemon grinned widely, and I swear his teeth were pointed again. "*Mae minima domina.* My name is Morax. I look forward to serving you, Michaela Bronwen."

The way my name sounded on his tongue set off little fireworks all over my body. I wasn't entirely sure what the other words he spoke actually meant. His accent was strange when he spoke the weird version of Latin. I needed to cool down this exchange and collect my thoughts fast.

"Great, um, Morax. So, my father is in deep shit with this crazy ass cult. They murdered my mother and my sister. And I know they have plans for me too. I have no intention of getting murdered or whatever else they want with me."

Morax's eyes darkened, and he snarled like a damn beast. "I will not let that happen."

I nodded. "Yes, that's why I summoned you." I turned

away from him, needing some space from the heat building between his body and mine. "So, what do we do now? Can we just kill them all?"

Morax chuckled as he circled me like a predator. "Have you killed someone before, *mae domina*?"

I squeezed the handle of the knife still in my hand, needing the reassurance of a weapon. Not that it would do much. He didn't seem intimidated, even when I pressed the blade to his throat.

I shook my head. "No. But these assholes murdered half my family and scattered the rest of us. They deserve to die, and I want to help."

Morax brushed a stray hair from my face, and I forced my body not to shiver again at his electric touch. "So fierce for one so breakable. I will help you get vengeance, Michaela. But I require something in return."

The hairs on the back of my neck stood in alarm. "What do you mean? Don't you just…have to do what I say?"

His eyes blazed bright gold, and his skin shimmered red. "A daemon is not a slave. And I am no ordinary daemon. You will owe me a debt, Michaela."

I didn't love the sound of that, but what choice did I have? If this daemon was strong enough to take on The Obscuritas, I would do just about anything to make that happen. "Fine."

Morax stepped close to me, his arm snapped out, and within seconds, he had my knife in hand. He examined it for a moment and smirked. "You won't be needing this. It wouldn't pierce my skin in daemon-form, anyway."

My limbs locked up with uncertainty as he dropped to one

knee in front of me. His head was almost level with my own as he knelt before me. I felt like a spirit watching this happen from above and unable to move. His hands moved up my thigh and under the long skirt of my dress. It was late September in South Carolina and the humidity was completely unbearable in anything but a dress. We were having an unnaturally long and hot summer. His fingers drifted further up my legs, and I swallowed, unsure what he would do but too curious to stop him. Only one guy had ever touched me like this, but I couldn't remember feeling so turned on—or terrified—like I was now. Morax lifted the fabric to reveal the leather strap wrapped around my thigh where I kept my blade. He slipped the knife into its case and dropped my skirt.

It was probably the single most sensual moment of my life. My cheeks heated at the thought, and I was grateful for the cover of night.

Morax remained on his knees as he took my hand and turned my palm up. His other hand shimmered, and the claws appeared once more. "This will only hurt a little."

I nodded, flattening my lips and refusing to show fear. "I can handle it."

Morax laughed deep in his chest, and some new emotion I couldn't name darkened his bright eyes. "I do not doubt it, feisty girl."

His claw dug into my skin, and I tried not to wince as blood pooled in my palm. He leaned forward, and before I could move, the daemon's tongue darted out to lick up the blood. I gasped as his forked tongue lapped at my bleeding hand. All I could think of were the stories of the devil and his forked tongue. So that little fairy tale was true. Morax let go of my hand, and I remained still while he clawed a line down his own palm. He stood, towering over me as his bloody hand drew closer to my mouth.

"I will protect you, Michaela Bronwen Valdis. And when the time comes, you will repay your debt in whichever way I choose. I swear this on the joining of our blood." His words echoed with power, and I knew this was the beginning of something wild. Something dangerous. Something that was all mine.

I looked into his eyes and gripped his wrist, my fingers unable to fully circle it. I swear he shivered at my touch. "I swear to honor my debt."

I slid my tongue out tentatively and licked at the cut in his palm. Morax groaned, and I gasped as the blood slipped down my throat. The brush of electricity I felt before was nothing compared to this. My veins were on fire, and I moaned at the ecstasy of that feeling. The feeling was more euphoric than any orgasm I had ever had. Every inch of me tingled with a burning need for more, and I could almost feel that desire mirrored in the monster before me. *What the hell did I just do?*

CHAPTER FOUR

Morax

I might have tricked her into blood-sharing, but when I realized this little lumen girl was my mate, I nearly lost control. Blood-sharing was not uncommon for daemons. And the only requirement was the offer had to be given freely, the blood could not be taken by force. When Michaela offered hers to me, my soul began to sing with desire. It took every ounce of my willpower not to take her back to my home and breed her until every inch of her milky white skin was marked with my scent. She was the most beguiling thing I had ever encountered.

When Michaela's blood hit my tongue, my cock was so fucking hard and my mind screamed with a possessive need so intense I groaned out loud. She didn't even look frightened when she spoke the words and leaned in to consume my blood. As soon as she did, I felt every emotion dancing through her. Fear. Curiosity. Desire. The last one nearly sent me to my knees again. She was perfect in every way. And she was all mine.

I never expected to find a mate. It was rare for daemons, and for a daemon and lumen to be mated was almost unheard of. My brother Phen would have a field day with this news. He told me it would happen, that I would find a mate in this human world, but I refused to believe him.

"Wait."

The change of her tone pulled me out of my rabid thoughts.

"What did you call me?" Her voice was barely a whisper.

I smiled. "Valdis. Your mother's family name."

She attempted to back away, but I held her wrist tightly to keep her close. She would never be rid of me.

Michaela sighed, absorbing this information quickly. "I guess I shouldn't be surprised you know who I am."

I chuckled, and pride filled my veins. She would need this strength in the months to come. My beautiful mate stared down at her palm, and we both watched as the wound began to heal.

Michaela smiled and held out her free hand. "A little gift from my mother. I'm a fast healer."

I cocked my head, curious. "How much do you know about Aurora?"

She shrugged, her golden hair shimmering in the moonlight. "More now than I ever did before. She didn't tell us anything. Well, at least not outright. My mother told us strange bedtime stories that I suspect are more than that. But I only learned she was something more than human after she was killed."

"She was a lumen. Akin to what the mortals think of as angels. She was exceptional. Royal. Half of your blood is that of a queen's."

Her blue- and honey-colored eyes grew round beneath dark lashes, and I ate up her undivided attention. She frowned, and instantly I wanted to take away the pain.

"I guess that makes sense. Otherwise this stupid cult wouldn't give a shit about me or my sisters."

I nodded, because this was mostly true, and smirked at her dirty mouth. "So crass, *mae domina*. But, yes. Your eldest sister was a full-blooded lumen and heir to the throne. The stories became hazy after her birth. There was much fighting among her people. Not unlike what my own people dealt with at the time. A prophecy came to us, and it was said a child born of a lumen and a daemon would rule us all. The lines between daemons and lumens began to blur as those in power sought to create such a powerful child."

Michaela crossed her arms. "What does that have to do with us, though?"

She really had no idea the trouble she was in. "Your other sister, Seraphina, is believed to be that child. These…what do you call them? Obscuritas? They are working with my brother to find her and use her to take control of your world—and ours."

Michaela let out a heavy sigh and ran her fingers through her long hair. I ached to do the same. "Well, that sucks."

I laughed, the nonchalant response catching me off guard. I was positively enthralled by this woman. "Yes, I suppose it does."

Michaela shivered, and I reached out to sense her feelings, realizing the damp air of the early morning was making her cold. I wasn't wearing a shirt and did not have a cloak to offer her. I wrapped one arm around her shoulders. "Come. I will return you to your home before anyone realizes you are gone. Tomorrow, I will arrive as your new personal bodyguard. Your father will believe he hired me."

She nodded, absorbing my words as we walked out of the woods and toward the small cabin she shared with her father.

There was more she needed to know about her situation,

and I growled possessively before uttering my next words. "There is more, Michaela."

Her head snapped up at my tone. "What is it?"

I sighed, but from her reactions thus far, I was certain she could handle this information. "The Obscuritas will come for you and your father. And you will go with them. It will become known I was a plant, working for this cult. It is the only way to infiltrate them and for me to remain by your side."

Michaela stopped walking and frowned up at me. "Why? Why can't you just kill them all now?"

I smiled down at her, letting my teeth sharpen as I held her petite face in my hands. "I will, *mae domina*. But there is so much more to this than you know. I need you to trust me. For now."

She stared back at me, and I swear her pretty eyes could see directly into the darkness of my soul. I wanted to tell her everything. Every secret I ever had. Tell her she was mine, my mate for eternity. But she was not ready for all of that. And I could wait. For her, I could wait.

CHAPTER FIVE

Michaela

When Morax brought me back to the small cabin I shared with my father, I almost asked him to stay with me. Almost. The words were right there, on the tip of my tongue. But before I could speak, he told me he would be nearby and all I had to do was call his name and he would come. The idea that a daemon would come to my aid just by saying his name was beyond thrilling. It was like having a pet. A big, scary, sexy pet.

I won't deny, I checked him out multiple times, but who wouldn't? Morax should honestly never wear shirts. Even as a human, his broad chest rippled with muscles. His arms were covered in tattoos of strange words and symbols I didn't recognize, all connected by vines licked by flames, disappearing over his shoulders and continuing down his back. His body was a work of art in more ways than one.

My cheeks flushed as I undressed and continued to picture my hot as shit daemon. The windows were open, and a breeze made me shiver as I stood naked, staring up at the moonlight. My nipples ached, and I brushed my hands over the pebbled peaks, flicking them absently as I wondered what my daemon was doing. I slid one hand down my belly and between my thighs. The soft hairs tickled my skin as I slipped a finger through my pussy. I was soaking wet. Dripping.

Living the way we did, sex and dating were not allowed. I was a virgin. A very curious and needy virgin. I didn't want to be, but how was I supposed to find someone? I allowed one guy to touch me, once. But it didn't feel right. I stopped things before we got close to sex.

I crawled into my small bed and propped up my legs, spreading them wide. My hand slipped between my legs again. My eyes fluttered as I toyed with my clit, a vision of Morax and his forked tongue filling my head. What would it feel like to have him down there? My legs began to shake as I circled my clit over and over. I dipped one finger inside my pussy and moaned at the feeling, imagining it was Morax and his wicked tongue probing me. The fingers of my other hand curled in the cotton sheets as I drew closer and closer to my orgasm. I bit my lip, forcing back a moan in an attempt to keep quiet in our tiny home.

I wondered what his cock looked like. Was it the same as a human's? I plunged two fingers inside my pussy, working myself and imagining it was his daemon cock stretching me, filling me. My body shook as the orgasm spread from my clit, down to my toes, and back. I slumped against the bed, sweat coating my skin. My eyes stayed closed as my mind continued to imagine the things Morax could do with his tongue. I begged my brain to let me dream of him instead of the nightmares as I surrendered to my exhaustion.

Whispers pulled me from my sleep. I heard my father's worried voice first. His general mood always landed somewhere between worry and sadness. Something broke inside him when my mother died. She was the only woman he had ever loved, ever married. Not that he couldn't get a new partner. He was a handsome man. Approximately six feet tall and olive skinned. My one brown eye came from him. The chestnut color of our eyes was flecked with gold and looked almost wolf-like. When Joseph Bronwen first met Aurora Valdis, she said his eyes drew her in first. And he teased her, replying that her sky-blue eyes were the real treasure, prettier than a cloudless summer day. My other eye was like hers. It was called heterochromia, when someone had two different colored eyes. When I was young, I pretended my eyes were unique because I was secretly a superhero. Not exactly accurate.

My father was speaking to someone and sounded increasingly anxious. It used to bother me when I was little, how sad and stressed he was all the time. I would cry alone in my room, wishing for my mother and sisters to come back. We both wished for them. Eventually, I stopped crying. But he never stopped being sad. I ignored his melancholy moods now, because what I had planned required strength and determination. He might not have faith in our future, but I wasn't ready to give up.

The voices continued as I slipped out of bed and quickly changed into a white lace thong and matching bra. I picked out a pair of cut-off jean shorts and a hot-pink T-shirt with a Deadmau5 logo on it. Any kind of house music, electronic, anything you'd hear at a rave, that was my jam. It was incredibly easy to sneak away from my father, and by the time I was sixteen, abandoned warehouse parties and raves were my happy places. The rush of adrenaline when the bass dropped and the crowds of people danced together calmed my soul. I could get lost in a crowd like that. Not one person knew who I was or what crazy ass shit was going on in my world. Just thinking about it had me itching to escape again. I was definitely addicted to the feeling.

I crept down the short hallway in bare feet toward the voices. When I finally focused my attention on the sounds, my throat dried up. I knew that voice. Morax was in my fucking living room chatting with my father. When I entered the room, his eyes were already trained on the doorway, like he could hear my silent steps moving toward them. My father turned, clearing his throat nervously.

Morax was dressed like a cop with a gun at his hip and a bulletproof vest. Gone were the horns and fangs and claws. He was in human form, still tall and muscular as shit, but slightly less intimidating to humans. I honestly preferred his daemon form. Red flushed my cheeks at the thought, and his lips twitched, hiding a smirk.

"Ah, D-Daughter," Joseph stuttered, clearly uncomfortable. "This is Mr., um, what was it again?"

Morax stepped around my father and into my personal space. I craned my neck to look at him. Damn, he was gorgeous. He winked down at me, his back facing my father, so only I could see his fangs descending when he grinned.

"Officer Axel Morgan. Pleasure to meet you, Michaela."

His deep voice did things to my insides, and I swallowed, dragging my teeth against my bottom lip. Morax tracked the movement. His eyes roamed over my face, my arms, down my bare legs, and back up again.

I crossed my arms over my chest. "Not really sure if it *is* a pleasure, Officer Morgan. What are you doing here?"

Morax took a step back and turned, speaking to my father again. "I was just relaying to your father that there was a break-in at a house down the road. The criminal escaped. We are checking the area. You haven't seen anyone?"

I shook my head. "Nope."

Morax raised an eyebrow. "Well, be sure to keep your doors and windows locked. I know the summer heat is still with us, but I wouldn't want this violent offender climbing in your window. Perhaps hearing sounds he couldn't resist."

His last words had my mouth dropping open. He heard me last night? *Oh, gods.* My face flushed, and I immediately walked across the living room to the kitchen and busied myself getting a glass of water.

My father finally spoke, cutting the tension he was so completely oblivious to. "Thank you, Mr., uh, Officer Morgan. We appreciate your coming here and will keep an eye out for anyone suspicious. It would mean a lot if you could personally check in on us and watch over my daughter."

I almost spit out the water I was gulping down. That last bit must be a joke. Morax made him say that. Father would never trust a stranger like that. I chugged down the rest of the glass of water, feeling Morax's eyes drilling into my backside. It was too hot in here. My skin was on fire, and I needed to get the hell out of this damn house. I placed the glass in the sink and turned to my father, ignoring the giant, sexy daemon elephant in the room.

"Father. I'm going to run to the store. We're out of…fruit. Need anything?" I walked over to the front door, slipped on my high-tops, and grabbed my purse.

"Michaela, I don't think it's a good idea to go out right now." My father frowned, wringing his hands. "I will go with you."

I rolled my eyes. "I'll be fine. I'm just going to the grocery store. Lots of people. And I have my pepper spray."

Morax shoved his hands in his pockets and walked toward me. "I will escort you. I should get back to the station."

I crossed my arms. "I don't need an escort. I'm sure you have more important things to do."

He smiled, and my insides melted. "It's no trouble at all. I will wait for you outside." His words left no room for discussion.

Morax walked out of the house, perfectly pleased with himself, and I ground my teeth. Father frowned at me and shook his head. I could see the confusion at this new situation stirring in the back of his mind.

"Michaela, I don't know about this. Let me just get some things together and I will go with you."

I squeezed my father's hand reassuringly. "Please don't worry. I will be back in under an hour."

Before he could reply, I scurried out the door and turned to my super annoying escort. Morax opened the passenger door of a police truck and stepped aside. I stuck my tongue out at him as I grabbed the handle and pulled myself up into the seat.

"Adorable." Morax chuckled before shutting the door and walking to the other side. He was almost too big for the damn truck.

"So, did you steal this?" I crossed my arms and leaned away from him.

Morax grinned, clearly pleased with himself. "Not exactly. Human minds are so malleable. I merely convinced the chief of police I was a new transfer, and he gave me the truck."

I couldn't help the smile on my face. "Bravo. Now what? How does *you* being a police officer help us?"

Morax started the truck before responding. "Did you know there is a low level member of The Obscuritas working in the police department? Two, actually. The admin and one of the officers."

My palms began to sweat, and I gripped the door handle, ready to bolt. Morax leaned over and gripped my wrist, pulling my arm away from the door. His touch sent a burst of heat straight across my belly.

He continued to hold my arm, using the other to drive us into town. "Relax, little lumen. As I said, human minds are fragile and easy to manipulate. Those two are fools. They have no idea you are here. They are more focused on fucking in the evidence room."

My rigid limbs relaxed slightly. I tried to pull my arm away, but Morax continued to hold my wrist, his arm across my chest like a seatbelt. His thumb traced the underside of my wrist, and I swore he could feel the rapid pulse beneath his touch.

"Speaking of fucking..." Morax growled, and I turned my head fully away from him and faced the window. "Look at me, little lumen."

I knew my cheeks were bright red, but he was the one that should be embarrassed. He was the one eavesdropping.

CHAPTER SIX

Morax

She turned to face me, and my smile widened when she obeyed my command. My mind filled with ideas, the commands I wanted to give her growing more depraved by the second. She brought this on herself, though. The rush of blood creeping up her creamy white skin at my words made my cock twitch. I wanted to eat her up. The constant tornado of emotions flowing from her mind was becoming my new favorite addiction. I couldn't read her mind like the humans; her lumen bloodline was strong. But I could get a general read of her emotions. My mate was equal parts angry and embarrassed. And aroused.

When I crept into the woods near her home last night, I intended to check on her before I went into town to spy on the stupid humans. It was nearly 2 a.m., and she should've been sleeping. But as I stalked nearer to her window, I heard something else. Not the gentle breathing of a sleeping princess, but moans of pleasure. I slipped beneath her open window, keeping my body low and out of the light of the moon. Her moans were soft and steady, her heartbeat beginning to race.

My ears picked up sounds far greater than a human, and I could hear her wet fingers plunging into her tight little cunt.

I ripped down my pants and immediately began stroking my cock. It took all my strength not to charge through the window and fuck her into oblivion. She wasn't ready for that. So instead, I stroked my cock aggressively as her moans grew louder and her fingers fucked her wet pussy more fiercely. I could smell her arousal in the air. My tongue flicked out, practically able to taste her. Her bed creaked as she moved, her body squirming under the assault of her fingers. She was close, and so was I. When she moaned my name, so softly no human could have heard her, hot cum shot out of my cock and I groaned.

The memory of her moaning my name was enough to get me hard all over again, and my grip on her wrist tightened. "Tell me, princess, did you enjoy your orgasm?"

Her face turned a beautiful shade of red, but her pretty eyes didn't flinch. "Yes."

I chuckled, and my cock throbbed. "So did I."

She scoffed at me. "You're a pervert. Creeping around and listening at people's windows."

"Not people"—I squeezed her arm—"just yours."

She liked that answer; I could taste her arousal in the air. I pulled the truck off the main road back to town and into a small clearing in the woods.

"What are you doing?" Michaela whispered. She licked her lips, and I resisted the urge to snatch her tongue.

I parked the truck and let go of her wrist. Turning in my seat, I gripped her chin and forced her to look at me. "I want you to show me."

Michaela's eyebrows scrunched together. "Show you what?"

I brushed my thumb across her lip, a satisfied purr building in my chest when her eyes dilated. "Show me how you make yourself come, princess."

Her eyes widened, and she tried to pull away, but I held her chin firmly between my fingers. She was so petite, I could snap her slender neck in an instant.

"I am not doing that." Her voice shook, but she was not afraid.

I could feel her desire even as she tried to deny me. But I would not be denied this. "You teased me with your pretty moans, princess. Did you know, just before your orgasm, you called out my name?"

Her mouth popped open, and I seized the opportunity to fill it with two of my fingers. She tried to pull away, but I gripped her throat with my other hand. "Relax. Suck."

Michaela's pupils dilated with desire, and I knew she could see the same heat mirrored in my own. Her tongue tentatively licked at my fingers, and my cock swelled at her compliance.

"Have you ever sucked a cock, Michaela?" I pushed my fingers further into her mouth, and her eyes watered as she resisted the urge to gag.

She nodded her head, and rage bubbled inside my chest. I pulled my fingers from her mouth. "Tell me."

She licked her lips and swallowed. My other hand remained wrapped around her pretty throat, stroking her pulse.

"Once. In high school, when we lived in Maine. I was in a regular school for a total of four months. Obscuritas members are everywhere, and my father grew increasingly paranoid." Michaela spoke softly, several emotions warring for dominance in her mind. "I was in the school play, *A Midsummer Night's*

Dream. I was one of the fairies, and he played Puck. His name was Sam and he was, predictably, a popular boy. I thought I liked him at the time. So, when he asked me to suck his cock backstage, I did it. It really wasn't that exciting. And I spit out his cum on the floor after he walked away."

If I could read her mind, I would have plucked the prick's last name from her thoughts, found the little idiot, and removed his head from his neck. I was exceedingly jealous. And spitting mad at his treatment of her. My mate.

I couldn't hold back the snarl of possessiveness. "I am very close to murdering the little shit, princess."

She laughed, and her arousal grew stronger at my threat. "He's not worth the trouble."

I squeezed her throat in warning. "He treated you poorly, which is enough. And I want to erase any being from this world who has seen you naked or touched your body. I want to rip the memory of his existence from your mind."

The brave little lumen leaned closer to me, her eyes capturing mine as my grip on her throat tightened. "Then make me forget." She opened her mouth, and hunger for her exploded throughout my body.

My horns appeared and my teeth sharpened as I lost control of my human form. I pressed my thumb against her tongue, and she sucked it into her pretty mouth. "Tell me, princess. Have you fucked someone yet?"

She shook her head, and I thanked the stars. If another cock had been inside my mate, I might have actually burned this entire world to the ground.

"I am pleased to hear it." I pressed my thumb further into

her mouth, reaching the back of her throat. Michaela's eyes watered, and I smiled. "I'm going to fill your sweet cunt, this smart mouth, and eventually that tight little ass with my cock."

She nearly choked on my thumb, and her eyes widened. Her pupils were blown with desire. I chuckled, pleased with her reaction to my words. Her reactions to me.

"Not today, my naughty little lumen. Today you are going to show me how you make your pretty pussy leak with desire."

Michaela swallowed and whimpered around my thumb. I pulled it from her mouth and gave her a moment to breathe.

She pulled away without speaking, and I let her go. Michaela unbuttoned her tiny shorts and shimmied out of them. My mouth dried up at the scrap of white lace covering her pussy. I wanted to tear it away with my teeth. She reached down and pulled her shirt over her head, and my cock swelled at my brazen little mate. The matching lacy white bra barely covered her petite breasts, and her hardened nipples peeked through the lace. I desperately needed her tits in my mouth.

"Fucking hell, princess." I growled the words. "You're the most stunning creature I have ever seen."

Her cheeks flushed, and she smiled up at me. I leaned over and pinched one of her nipples. She yelped and swatted my hand, but I didn't move away.

"What the hell!" She squirmed and moaned as I pinched her nipple.

I let go and rubbed the pain away. "No one will ever see you like this. Only me. Understood?" The last word came out like a snarl, but I couldn't help it. I was growing ravenous.

Michaela smirked. "What about when I wear a bikini?"

I pinched her other nipple for the sass. "I'll consider it. Now take that little thong off. Your cunt is soaked, and I won't be able to restrain myself much longer."

My naughty mate laughed, and the sound made my cock throb. I loved how bold she was, even with the little experience she had. The thong slipped down her tan legs, and I snatched it from her hand. I brought the wet fabric to my nose and inhaled.

"Fuck, princess." I closed my eyes and groaned. My forked tongue snapped out to taste. "You are the most delectable thing I have ever tasted. And so fucking wet."

I opened my eyes to see her chest heaving as she slipped her delicate fingers between her legs. She moaned as she touched herself and watched me lick her thong.

"I want to see you." Her words were soft but confident. "I know you said we weren't going to fuck. But I want to see your cock. I want you to come too."

I grinned like the deranged daemon I absolutely was. "My little lumen has a filthy fucking mouth. It's going to get you in trouble."

Michaela pulled her hand away, and my own snapped out, stopping her.

"Do not stop until I say so."

She nodded, her fingers circling her clit once more.

I leaned over, bringing my face closer to her wet cunt. She was mostly shaved, with a small patch of golden hair. I wanted to bury my face in it.

"Spread your lips for me, princess. I need to see your cunt," I commanded, and like a good girl, she obeyed.

I growled, and my mouth watered as I stared at the most

beautiful pink pussy I had ever seen. She was soaked, her cream already leaking out of her tight cunt. I couldn't help myself. Leaning fully across the seat, I brought my head down between her legs. My tongue flicked out, and the taste of her juices enveloped my senses.

"Fuck." Michaela whimpered and squirmed as I flicked my tongue out again and circled her clit once. Twice.

I pulled away slowly, savoring her. "Princess, you taste like angel cake. I don't think I will ever get enough. I want the taste of your cunt on my tongue for eternity."

Michaela moved her fingers back to circle her clit and smiled like a sinner. "Now let me see you."

I chuckled but acquiesced. I unbuttoned my pants, and my very hard cock sprang out. Daemon and lumen anatomy was similar to humans, with a few enhancements. Daemon cocks were ribbed down the shaft, adding extra pleasure for our partners and for us. Daemons also often adorned their cocks and pussies with piercings and tattoos. I did not have either yet. It was something I wanted to do with my mate.

She gasped. "Oh, my gods. That is not going to fit."

My smirk turned into a dark laugh. "Oh, princess. It will fit. My cock was made for you."

I could tell she didn't quite understand what I meant, but now was not the time to tell her we were mated.

"How does your pussy feel, princess? How many fingers can you take for me?" I stroked my cock as I spoke softly to her.

Her eyes stayed glued to my movements as she inserted a second finger and moaned. "Two."

I squeezed the head of my cock, pre-cum seeping out. I

wouldn't last much longer. Being so close to my mate with her scent filling the truck was driving me insane. "One more, princess."

She obeyed. Her back arched as she fucked her little cunt with her fingers. She reached across the console slowly, and I was too curious to stop her. Her hand tentatively circled the base of my cock. She couldn't completely wrap her fingers around my girth. The positioning wasn't ideal either, sitting in the seats of the truck. But it was enough—for now.

Michaela looked up at me with her colorful eyes. "I want to feel it when you come."

I grinned at her, my bold mate. "Such a filthy little lumen." I reached over and flicked her clit with my thumb. "Fuck those fingers, princess. Don't hold back. I want to hear you moan my name again."

Michaela's moans grew louder as she fucked her hand and I toyed with her clit. Her other hand squeezed my cock, and I stroked faster. I could hear her heart racing as we both moved closer and closer to our orgasms. I whispered her name, and she moaned for me.

"Fuck. I'm gonna come," Michaela whimpered, her eyes still locked on my cock.

I moved my thumb faster, circling her clit in a steady motion. "Come for me, princess."

Her back arched and her legs shook as she came for me. "Morax. Fuck. Yes!"

Hearing my name on her lips sent me over the edge. Cum oozed out of my cock as I stroked slowly, trying not to shoot it everywhere. "Damn, princess."

My breathing was harsh as I praised her. The truck was fogging up with our heavy breaths, and the scent of sex filled the sticky air. I pulled my shirt over my head and leaned over to wipe up the mess she made.

Her face was shy as she watched me clean her up. I turned her chin up to look at me. "You are positively exquisite when you moan my name. I could listen to that sound forever. And I intend to do so over and over again."

Michaela blushed. "I think I'd like that too."

I grinned at her. She didn't have a choice, but we weren't getting into that now. I used my shirt to wipe up my own mess as she pulled her shorts back on. It was hot as fuck in here, so I cranked the A/C.

Michaela giggled, and I arched a brow at her. "I don't think you can go back to the station like that. And definitely not in the grocery store."

I winked at her. "Wait here."

She frowned but nodded. I stepped out of the truck and closed my eyes. Daemons and lumens had many convenient abilities, and one of them was a version of teleportation. I envisioned the grocery store, and moments later, found myself in the aisle I needed. I quickly took over the minds of any humans nearby so they wouldn't be able to see me. It was such a change from my own world. Controlling the minds of even lower daemons or lumens was occasionally difficult, but here I could snatch the thoughts out of dozens with minimal effort. I grabbed a basket and filled it with an assortment of fruits, cheeses, and bread, not having any idea what Michaela would like to eat. She was too skinny, though, and that was something

I would remedy quickly.

Once my basket was full, I closed my eyes and popped back into existence beside the truck. When I opened the door, Michaela was staring with her mouth open.

"How the hell did you do that?" She waved her hands in the air.

I laughed, delighting in her awe. "Perks of being a daemon, princess. I'm sure you will have some similar abilities, once you figure out how to access them."

Michaela crossed her arms and pouted. "Everything would be so much easier if I could do that."

I shook my head and placed the basket of food in the back seat. "Not necessarily. The Obscuritas have access to some magic. I suspect they could find you more easily if you were openly using your own power."

She leaned her arms on the console as I climbed into the truck. "Is that what you call it? Magic?"

My little lumen was so curious. And clueless. *Why did her mother keep our world secret from her own children?*

"What humans conjure up, we call magic. Akin to witches. There are witches in our world as well. They are a strange breed, descendents of some unknown god. The humans who are capable of magic, they will likely find one of our witches as an ancestor. Daemon and lumen power we call vis-el."

Michaela's face lit up with a thousand questions, and I reached over to smash her lips together before she could speak. "There will be time for history lessons. Now is not one of those times."

She rolled her eyes at me, and I had half a mind to spank

her ass raw for her sass. I released her mouth and drove her home instead. Now was not the time for that either.

"I wish my mother had told me all of this," she whispered, staring out the window. "She didn't even tell my father most of it. Or he didn't ask. I don't really know which."

The hurt in her voice made my grip tighten on the steering wheel. I hated her parents for making her sad. I wanted to bash her human father's head in for failing her so fully.

"I don't know what your mother's plan was for you or your sisters, but I do believe she had one." I glanced her way to see her strange, beautiful eyes watching me. "Aurora was the greatest seer of her lifetime. It may be difficult to believe, but I do not think she would leave you helpless. My presence here is proof of that."

Michaela scoffed, and her laugh tickled my ears. "When you start actually being useful, I'll consider that."

The growl that rumbled in my chest was nothing short of terrifying, but my mate didn't even flinch. We pulled up to the small cabin she shared with her father, and I grabbed the basket of food out of the truck for her. She tried to take it, but I simply held it above my head and out of her reach as I walked her to the front door.

"Will you do something for me, little lumen?" I set the basket on the bench beside the front door.

Michael crossed her arms. "Depends what it is."

I stepped closer to her until her back pressed against the front door. I let my horns grow and my eyes change color. Michaela sucked in a breath, but held my gaze.

"I need you to behave this evening. I am going to follow

some Obscuritas scum and I can't have my thoughts in two places while I hunt."

Her eyes widened. "Why not?"

I smirked down at her, envisioning a different kind of hunt. "You will find out soon enough."

My mate started to roll her eyes. I snatched her throat with my hand and squeezed. Her eyes bulged, but she said nothing. I pressed my thumb against her pulse to feel her heartbeat racing. Michaela glared back at me, and my tongue flicked out to lick her cheek. I chuckled as her nose scrunched up.

"Behave for me, princess. And I will show you how useful I can be." I whispered the words against her delicate ear and smiled when she shivered.

Before she could respond with a sassy comment that would definitely get her ass spanked, I let her go and walked back to the truck. If I didn't leave now, I would not be able to leave at all. Her scent changed as I held her life in my hands, and the smell of her arousal was going to drive me insane. I needed a clear head tonight. The humans were easy to manipulate, but to make them believe what I needed them to believe, my mind needed to be focused.

I could still taste her delicious cum on my fingers, and the smell of sex filled the truck. Driving away from her was akin to ripping out my heart, her power over me so encompassing already. But I would be back by morning, at the latest. She could handle herself for one night.

CHAPTER SEVEN

Michaela

I was absolutely *not* going to behave. All I ever did was behave. Lie low, listen to my father, don't make friends, don't do this and don't do that. I wasn't originally planning to sneak out tonight, but that little speech got my blood boiling. There was a warehouse party happening not too far away, and now that I was on the warpath to be very, very bad, I would be going to said party.

My father wouldn't notice. He rarely noticed when I snuck out. Or he did but didn't have the strength to stop me. Either way, it hurt. Every time he did nothing, it hurt. Sometimes I thought Seraphina was better off being on her own. At least she didn't have a parent sulking around and barely acknowledging her existence. After Father told me everything he knew about daemons and lumens and I got access to mother's books, he basically shut down. Like nothing mattered. Like I didn't matter.

And the only thing loud enough to drown out all the terrible feelings was music. Loud, pulsing, electronic music and sweaty bodies moving to the beat. Father wouldn't know I was gone, and neither would my daemon babysitter.

I made an easy pasta dinner for us then retreated to my room for the evening. This wasn't unusual. Before I knew all that I did now, we would have dinner together. He would smile at me and tell me bedtime stories. We would bake cookies together. He was everything to me. But as I grew older, I asked more questions about my sisters. My mother. And he hated giving me answers.

He did, though. I remember taking in all that information, trying hard not to run screaming from the crazy person telling tales. But I knew he wasn't lying. Some small corner of my mind remembered that night. The screams of my sister and my mother. The feel of the air, electric with some force, some otherworldly power.

Their screams still rang out in my nightmares. The music was the only thing that could drown them out. And since my ridiculous daemon left me for the night, to the party I would go.

I changed out of my jean shorts and T-shirt and pulled out a box from the back of my closet where I kept my rave clothes hidden. Not that Father would snoop, but I liked keeping this side of me a secret from everyone. I pulled out a bright-pink bra and matching boy shorts. Then I slipped a mesh, neon green bodycon dress over the set. I grabbed my high-top sneakers and slipped them on. I wasn't really interested in heels. But I loved the skimpy clothes and how the neon colors shown in the black lights. I curled my hair in soft waves, fluffing it up a bit with hairspray.

My hair wasn't thin, but it was fine and never looked as cool as my sisters'. Lailah and I had similar body types, long legs and slender frames, and our mother's blonde hair. Seraphina had more curves and better tits. She also had thick, beautiful red hair. I was always jealous of her looks.

After I finished applying my sparkly eyeshadow and hot-pink lipstick, I crept out of my room to check on Father. He was passed out in his recliner with some football game blaring on the TV. He would be there all night. I grabbed my purse and the keys to his Jeep then slipped out the door.

We only had one vehicle. The Jeep Wrangler was older, something from the early 2000s. Joseph Bronwen was a car mechanic when he first met Aurora Valdis. He had his own shop back in Maine. They met when she brought her car in for service. And the rest, as they say, was history. I suspect Aurora knew him already. How could such a pairing come about by chance?

The warehouse was only about thirty minutes from our town. We generally lived in smaller cities or rural towns, and this particular home we'd stayed in longer than any others, which meant I was able to make a handful of friends. I wasn't allowed to have a cell phone, but Father didn't know I kept a prepaid phone for this very purpose. Penny sent me the address for the party and details to get in. She was one of those girls who had connections everywhere. The parties always required tickets, but not for Penelope Lirakis, which worked out really well for me.

I parked my Jeep close to the exit of the massive parking lot. One of the things you learned being on the run and hiding from bad people was to always know your exits. I was familiar with this venue, as I had attended several raves here over the last two years. I knew all the building exits and best spots to park. I could hear the music and the base pulsing as I walked toward the building. There were dozens and dozens of people waiting in line to get in. It was always a rush to walk past them all and up to the two bouncers, one for checking the VIP list and one to be the "muscle."

I walked straight up to the bouncer with the clipboard. "Hi. I'm on the list. Lara Croft."

One of my favorite fictional characters of all time was Lara Croft from *Tomb Raider*. She was an absolute badass and took no shit. I aspired to be like her. The bouncer raised an eyebrow but said nothing. He looked down his round nose at the list and nodded to the meathead bouncer at his side. I grinned and saluted them as I skipped down the hall and into the warehouse. I passed people decorated in glowing body paint handing out glow stick necklaces and bracelets. I grabbed several of each, wrapping them around my arms and throat. There was a massive, makeshift bar along the far wall of the open floor warehouse. A second level held tables and couches for those who wanted to escape the dance floor. Not me, I thrived on the dance floor. Penny would be upstairs, though, so I found the staircase and made my way to the VIP area. She was holding court with a small group of people.

Penny was shorter than me and blessed with the perfect hourglass figure. She had long, dark, curly hair and green eyes. Not a single man or woman could deny she was gorgeous. We met, randomly, at a thrift store. Tonight, she wore a bright-blue, pleather bodycon dress. She paired the dress with Converse low-tops, which made me love her more. Penny could pull off some seriously high heels, but she was a sneakers girl at heart, like me.

She was mid-sentence when her eyes turned up and she

noticed my approach. She squealed and jumped up from her couch. "Lady Croft!"

I laughed as she barreled into me for a hug. Penny was the only friend who knew my real name. She didn't know all the crazy details, because how could you tell someone about daemons and lumens? But I told her a version of my story. She thought I was in Witness Protection because some crazy gang was after my family.

"I'm so glad you came!" Penny exclaimed, kissing my cheek and certainly leaving behind red lipstick.

I squeezed her hands and smiled at my friend. "Of course. How could I say no?"

She grinned. "Want to meet some people? There's an absolutely delicious boy over there I think you'd enjoy."

I shook my head and blushed, my thoughts immediately going to my daemon. "I'm ready to hit the dance floor."

"I'm going to find you a boy toy eventually, Lady Croft." Penny winked and turned to her group. "It's time to dance, y'all!"

The others stood, downing their cocktails as they walked by us.

Penny's arm snapped out and pulled a cute guy aside. "Gavin, meet my friend, Lara."

Gavin turned to me with a dimpled smile, and okay fine, he was cute. He had curly blond hair and pretty blue eyes. He looked like a surfer from California.

"Hey, Gavin. Nice to meet you." I stuck out my hand, and he took it instantly, lingering a little too long.

"Penny's been talking about you all night. Pleasure to finally meet you, Lara." Gavin's British accent caught me off guard.

Definitely not a surfer dude from California.

I laughed, because I had no doubt Penny did just that. Before I could respond, Penny grabbed my hand and ordered Gavin to follow us. The crowd parted as we made our way to the middle of the dance floor. The DJ spinning tonight was excellent. I closed my eyes and let the music take me away. My hips swayed to the beat, and I smiled, feeling some tiny bit of peace.

An arm wrapped around my middle, and my eyes popped open. For a split second, I thought it was Gavin and I was ready to push him off, because I preferred dancing on my own. But when I gripped the muscular arm and electric heat shot through my veins, I knew who was behind me. I looked straight ahead at Penny. Her mouth was wide and her green eyes were bulging, confirming what I already knew.

Morax was here.

CHAPTER EIGHT

Morax

For the hundredth time, I cursed the stars and asked them why I was linked to such a hellion of a mate. The little lumen did *not* behave as I had commanded her to do. No obedient daemon wife for me, apparently. If I was being honest, the thought of anyone else made me physically ill. I didn't want any of the boring daemons or lumens Father tried to force on me. I wanted her. My hybrid princess with more stubbornness than a hellhound.

It was just after 1 a.m., and I was finally finished melding the minds of the idiotic cult members. I discovered very little information from them. Only one member was helpful. Someone related to one of The Obscuritas Kings. He had a few secrets. Things about my little lumen's psycho sister. And one particularly upsetting secret about a daemon hunting for the daughters of Aurora Valdis.

Before Aurora used her life force to cut off access between our world and the human's Earth, the more powerful daemons and lumens could walk between worlds. When the wars started between our two species, most of the daemons and lumens returned home. A few stayed behind, cowards choosing to play like gods among the humans. The name I pulled from the cult member was one I knew very well. He was quite powerful. And loyal to my father. It would be no small task to take him out. Not that I couldn't. As strong as Gremory was, he was not of the royal bloodline and he did not possess enough power to defeat me.

Gremory was only two hundred years old, at least in human years. Daemons and Lumens aged differently than humans. We reached the human age of fifteen after a hundred years of existence. After the first hundred years, the aging process slowed significantly. By our two hundredth year, we stopped aging almost entirely. Only significant life events, or a very powerful witch, could cause us to age further. We could live for thousands of years. We were not immortal, but we were very difficult to kill. Only a handful of things in our world could kill us.

And I happened to bring one of those things with me from home—a blade made of stellatium. Stellatium was a metal created by the death of a star. Humans on Earth could find this rare metal as well, but without knowledge of our world, it would only look like strange rocks. In Caligo, my city, we had a guild of star hunters who constantly watched the skies and mined the stellatium. The lumens were susceptible to it as well, and there were often bloody fights to retrieve the precious metal when a star crashed between their city, Caelum, and ours.

I pulled the blade from its sheath. It was small, but I didn't need a broadsword to kill Gremory. A quick stab to the heart would do it. How I didn't sense his presence in this town immediately was still a mystery to me. He must be using a human witch to douse his power. I clasped an iron bracelet to my wrist and grimaced when the metal scorched my skin. The iron would dampen my own aura to keep him from sensing me. I extended a claw and cut a symbol into my forearm. As

my blood welled and dripped to the ground, I closed my eyes and sought out the daemon. He wasn't far. But he was too close to my mate.

My thoughts drifted once more to my little lumen, and I hoped she was not in his grasp yet. Their auras were too close, and rage simmered beneath my skin as I drove through the city streets and arrived at a warehouse that looked in dire need of repairs. Loud, pulsing music flooded my ears, and flashing lights illuminated the street. There was a long line of people dressed in wild attire. This was clearly a massive underground party of some kind.

I was not surprised to find my little lumen here. In the handful of days I'd known her, Michaela always had music playing. I couldn't help but listen in to see what she preferred. When she was trying to drown out the world, it was often dance and electronic music.

It was more troubling to find Gremory was inside as well. Was he here for her? Or was there another being I needed to worry about? My priority was Michaela. Once she was safe, I would torture, question, torture some more, and then kill Gremory. The torture bit could last quite some time, depending on what he had to say. And it would be incredibly painful.

I walked around the back of the building and let my wings snap out. Digging my claws into the ground, I shoved off and flew to the top of the building. There was no time for dealing with bouncers and lines of pathetic humans. The door on the roof was locked, and I used a bit of daemon strength to wrench it open. The stench of human sweat, marijuana, and alcohol assaulted my senses. I crept down the stairs and along a balcony overlooking the main dance area. There were others on this platform, hiding in corners and reeking of sex. I closed my eyes and centered my own senses, recalling my mates sweet smell and the lure of her blood.

She was at the center of the dance floor. I could feel the euphoria radiating off her skin. My little lumen was glowing, but it was so faint, no one would notice the ethereal color of her skin. Her eyes were closed as her body swayed to the steady pulse of the music. Her full lips were parted slightly, as if she were about to moan with pleasure. Her tongue slid out and licked those perfect lips, and I growled. I did not like my mate looking like a goddess in heat without me by her side. Several human males watched her dance, and it took all of my strength not to leap from this balcony and gouge out their eyes for leching after what belonged to me.

The lights flashed, and Michaela's hot-pink lingerie caught my eye. She looked fucking exquisite. The most delectable treat I couldn't wait to taste. And I was done waiting. I stalked down the steps, a snarl on my lips for anyone standing in my way. My dark-wash jeans and black T-shirt stood out more thoroughly in the sea of brightly colored clothing. I was a shadow, a dark abyss coming to devour my pretty mate.

I stalked up close behind her. The moment she sensed my presence her body tensed in alarm and I grinned. She stopped dancing, and I slid my arms around her waist possessively.

"Hello, princess."

Michaela didn't turn around, but she tilted her head to the side and peeked up at me through dark lashes. "Hi."

"Is this what you consider behaving?" I slid my fingers

along the edge of the silky little shorts she wore beneath the neon mesh dress. My claws extended slightly as my need for her grew, and I dug them into her skin, but only enough to tease.

She whimpered, and the sound was music to my ears. "Maybe."

I wanted nothing more than to haul her ass out of here and find a dark corner to fuck the brat right out of her, but there was another presence across the room I needed to deal with.

Michaela continued to dance, pushing her perfect little ass against my thigh. She wasn't quite tall enough to grind her ass against the semi I was now sporting, but I pulled her tightly against my chest and she gasped when my cock pressed into her lower back.

I leaned down and nipped at her ear. "We have a problem. And while I'd like nothing more than to bend you over and spank your ass until it turned as red as a cherry, it will have to wait. There is another daemon here."

Michaela's breath hitched, and she turned to face me.

I grabbed her arms and draped them around my neck. My rough hands circled her waist as I leaned down close enough for her to hear me speak. "Keep dancing. I don't know why he is here. But he does not seem to be watching you. He will, though, if I stay with you."

"What should we do?" She looked up at me with wide eyes, unafraid. My cock thickened at the sight.

"You will stay here and dance with your friend. *No* males."

She rolled her eyes, and my hand snapped out to grab her chin.

"I mean it. I can make your punishment more pleasurable,

or more painful. Behave while I handle the daemon. Do not leave this area. Understood?"

My little lumen pouted but nodded. "I'll behave. But what if *they* don't behave? I can't control other people."

I tapped her temple. "Someday you will be able to." I took her hand and brought her wrist to my nose, smelling the sweet blood pulsing in her veins just beneath the surface of her delicate skin. My tongue slid out and licked her pulse. The beat of her heart jumped, and I groaned at how quickly her body responded to my touch. I nipped her palm and kissed her fingers. Her pupils were blown wide with desire, and her mouth parted slightly.

I kissed her wrist once more. "You are the most beautiful creature I have ever seen. Now be a good girl for me and I will finish what I started."

Michaela licked her lips and nodded, making me smile and practically purr with satisfaction.

I let her go, reluctantly, and headed toward the bar across the room. Gremory was easy enough to spot. He sported his signature bright blonde hair, tied back at the nape of his neck. His sky-blue eyes shown brightly even in the dark warehouse. Several men and women stared at him with lust in their own eyes as he mixed cocktails for them with inhuman flair. He wore a terrible shiny silver shirt and dark jeans, an attempt to blend in. I could see the glow of his skin as he subtly lit the alcohol on fire and blew it down a row of shots until the entire bar was aglow. The humans were dumb and drunk, otherwise the unnatural fire would be obvious. I could read the uncertainty flickering in the minds of a few of them, but none spoke up.

Gremory caught my eye, and a flash of fear passed across his face before he expertly hid it away.

"Hello, Grem."

"Well, hello, wayward prince." Grem mock bowed, and I nearly launched at him across the bar. The gaul of this lesser daemon to mock me so openly was mildly impressive.

I leaned across the bar, and the humans scattered as I convinced them to find another bartender. "I've killed daemons for lesser crimes. Would you like to try that again?"

Grem smiled but didn't balk at the threat, nor did he address me properly. "And what brings you here, Son of Corson? I had no idea you left Caligo."

I eyed the daemon warily. No one could come to Earth because of Aurora's shield. He knew this, which meant he also knew I had found one of her descendents to break the barrier, because I was still in Caligo when the initial ritual occurred. But did he know Michaela was here? Or had he found Seraphina?

"The extent of my power is great, and it does not surprise me you lack the knowledge or know-how to travel between worlds." I drawled on, hoping to distract him enough to enter his mind, but his shields were solid. Not that I expected them to be weak, but it would have made this a lot easier. "Let us speak somewhere quieter."

Grem mock-bowed again, and I snarled. He ignored me and proceeded to walk down the length of the bar and toward an exit. I followed him. Every fiber of my being wanted to glance back at Michaela, but the moment I almost gave in, I felt eyes on me. Someone else was watching us. And I refused to let them see her.

CHAPTER NINE

Michaela

I really was trying to behave, but when Morax followed a not-so-human-looking guy to the back of the warehouse and another not-so-human-looking guy followed *them*, things changed. Morax wasn't helpless; he was probably the least helpless being here. But when I saw that second guy following and caught the glint of a weapon sticking out of the back of his pants, something feral woke inside me. I couldn't let him go alone.

Penny was still dancing and oblivious to the tension building inside me, but she was also on drugs, so I forgave her. I slipped off the dance floor, saying I had to pee, and darted away before she could follow me. Morax and the two strangers must've gone outside, because the hallway I turned down was empty and dark. The glow sticks wrapped around my wrists and neck were like a damn beacon, so I quickly ripped them off and stuffed them into a trash bin. My outfit didn't have many places to hide a weapon, but I never left the house unprepared. The slim blade hidden in my bra would have to do.

The sound of harsh voices grew louder as I crept down the hall and came to an exit. The glass window next to the door was cracked and covered in dust, so I couldn't see much.

I peeked between the broken pieces of glass and sucked in a breath. Morax had several cuts on his arms and one across his chest. He stood casually, as if the two creatures in front of him, crouched and ready to attack, were no threat at all.

"Come now, Grem," Morax mused. "Have you stooped so low as to refuse a one-on-one fight? And you're working with a fucking lumen?"

"Fuck you, royal trash!" the one who followed Morax screeched, and a burst of light shot out from his hands.

Morax deflected it easily and my heart raced as I gaped openly at the power he wielded. His horns grew, and his black feathered wings opened slowly, their long shadow reaching the two men. His claws extended, and the glint of his fangs made a shudder run through my body.

"Try that again, and I will cut your fucking hands off and feed them to you," Morax snarled.

The power emanating from my daemon made my knees weak. How the other two were still standing, I had no idea.

"Ouriel." The other daemon growled his name. At least, I assumed he was a daemon. He had similar feathered wings, although his were a deep shade of green, and horns too. He wasn't quite as impressive as Morax, though. "We are here to talk. No need to start flashing lights about."

The one called Ouriel scoffed, crossing his arms. He did not have wings, but his skin was glowing a light blue, and I could feel power radiating off of him, even from my hiding place.

Morax smirked at the daemon. "Yes, let's be civil about this, Gremory. What exactly are you doing for my father with these humans?"

The one called Gremory chuckled, his eyes twinkling. "Oh, silly prince. You don't know? I don't work for your father."

This news seemed to startle my daemon. His eyes narrowed as he stared at Gremory.

"Belial?" Morax whispered the name, a low growl building in his chest.

"Belial is the true king. He will unite our people and those who are loyal will be rewarded." Ouriel professed the words proudly like some lovesick idiot.

Gremory rolled his eyes. Before I could register the movement, he threw a dagger and it sunk deep into the lumen's chest. Ouriel's eyes widened with shock, and then he was gone. His body burst into thousands of tiny sparks that instantly shot into the sky, and it was like the lumen was never there at all. The blade dropped to the ground, the only evidence of the entire exchange.

"Gods, he was annoying. Ouriel was sucking your asshole brother's cock before Belial sent him here to kill you." Gremory smirked and sauntered over to the fallen blade.

In the next instant, Morax launched another knife. Gremory barely got his arm up in time to block the blade from reaching his heart. The daemon snarled and ripped the knife out of his forearm, throwing it back in Morax's direction. My daemon side-stepped easily and ran at him. Both daemons dropped to the ground as they fought, snarling, scratching, and biting.

I wanted to help, wanted to do something, but all I could do was watch as these creatures of myths and legends fought like beasts. Gremory was a dirty fighter. Right away, I could tell Morax was stronger, but the slippery daemon kept evading him. He taunted Morax, talking about his family and all the secret plans they had. My daemon snarled and glared at him, his blade slashing out over and over.

Gremory rolled away and picked up the blade he had dropped earlier, and a strangled sound escaped me as he prepared to throw it. My cry was enough to startle the daemon and his head snapped in my direction. I froze, and seconds later Morax had a dagger piercing through the other daemon's chest. Gremory roared in pain and shoved Morax away. His wings flapped, blowing up dust, and he launched into the sky.

Morax dropped to his knees, and I bolted through the door and ran to him. As soon as I reached him, his arm snapped out and his hand wrapped around my throat. I gasped, my eyes wide as I stood rigid and unsure. Morax glared at me with glowing, golden eyes. His clawed fingers pressed into my neck and restricted my airflow. My breaths hitched as he squeezed. He snarled and stood before me, so impossibly large. I should have been afraid, but I wasn't.

Slowly, I pressed my hands to his chest. His shirt was torn to shreds, and I slipped my fingers beneath it and ran my hands up his chiseled abs. Morax growled, but this one was softer and less scary, so I continued with my soft touches. Black spots were popping up in my vision from lack of oxygen as my fingers reached his face. I cupped his cheek and tried to whisper his name.

The heat radiating from his skin dimmed, and his hold on my throat lessened enough for me to suck in a few shallow breaths. Morax bowed his head.

"I thought they were going to find you. I knew you were

there from the moment you crept down that hallway, little lumen." He whispered the words, his voice shaking with anger. "I was desperate to keep their attention away from you. Away from your scent."

My eyes widened. "I'm sorry. I saw the second one follow you and I just couldn't let you go alone."

Morax smirked. "My fierce princess, coming to my rescue." His hand loosened around my throat, and he stroked my pulse. "You are in so much trouble."

I nodded. "I know."

He stooped down suddenly, and his hands gripped my thighs and pulled me up until my legs wrapped around his waist. He walked us toward the woods, away from the warehouse filled with people grinding to the music. Morax shoved me against a tree roughly and dropped his mouth to my neck. I moaned as he licked and sucked his way up to my ear.

"Grem escaped. My blade didn't pierce his heart," Morax murmured against my skin. "He will run back to his human masters and tell them I am here."

I moaned again as he grinded against my body. My mesh dress slipped up over my thighs, and the thin silk of my little booty shorts was barely a barrier. The rough fabric of his jeans brushed against my center over and over until I was practically panting for him to fuck me.

Morax paused his steady assault, and I whimpered, missing the friction.

"However. When you cried out and distracted him, I saw into his mind enough to know where he was going. He will heal first, and then go to The Obscuritas Kings. But I will find him before then."

His words sunk into my sex-addled brain.

"Do you have to go now, then?"

Morax chuckled, and the sound was positively filthy. "No, princess. Not just yet. But my need to hunt must be satiated." He stepped back and circled around me like a predator.

I felt his gaze on me, stalking me. "Hunt? What do you need to hunt, like a deer?"

Morax smirked, his golden eyes glowing in the darkness. "Yes, like a deer. A pretty little doe with mismatched eyes."

My breathing stalled as I finally understood what he was saying. "You want to hunt me?"

He stepped close once more, and his claws curled beneath my chin, turning my face up to his. "More than anything."

I licked my lips, and Morax zeroed in on the small movement.

He tilted his head to the side, eying me like a rare steak he intended to devour. "I'll give you a head start. And I won't even use my wings."

My thighs clenched, and his nostrils flared, scenting my arousal.

I crossed my arms, needing to do something with my hands. "What happens if you don't catch me?"

He grinned like a cocky asshole, but fuck, he was gorgeous when he smiled like that. "If I don't catch you, choose your prize."

Immediately, I knew what I wanted and smiled. "You come with me to another warehouse party. Only this one is a paint party."

"Done," Morax responded instantly, still sporting that devastating smile. His horns appeared, and his claws traced delicate circles across my chest.

My breaths grew more shallow as he teased me. His fangs descended, and I bit my bottom lip. "What do you get if you catch me?"

He leaned in, his mouth centimeters away from my own. "When I catch you, I'm going to devour you."

I gasped, and he chuckled. The sound was terrifying and heated my entire body with need.

"Run, little doe. Now."

I didn't need to be told twice. I turned and fled into the forest. Thank fucking goodness I wore sneakers. They weren't exactly the kind to traipse through a forest in, but they were better than heels. In horror movies, the girls were always in heels.

Was this a horror movie? My heart beat a million miles an hour as I ran for my life, but I felt…exhilarated. And really damn horny. Was this a thing, getting hot for a crazy daemon chasing you through the woods?

I swiped at low branches, taking the tiny scratches as I ran. I didn't slow down. Maybe I wanted him to find me, but I sure as hell wasn't going to make it easy.

The cabin Father and I lived in was surrounded by woods, and I'd been exploring them for the few years we lived there. I liked walking through the forest at night and listening to the creatures come alive. This was no different, except now one of those creatures was chasing me. I took a sharp left, hearing the sound of water. There was a small stream ahead. Crossing it might help cover my scent. It wasn't too wide. I took a few steps back and leapt over it. I lost my footing and fell on my ass with a yelp on the far side. *Shit.*

I scrambled to my feet and started running again, my muscles burning, but I couldn't stop. Morax likely heard me fall. One of the many powers I read about in my mother's books was the naturally heightened senses of both daemons and lumens. This was so not fair. I ran for another minute then ducked behind a thick oak tree to catch my breath.

When I stopped, my heart nearly dropped out of my ass. The forest was silent. I couldn't hear a single creature stirring, and that could only mean one thing. There was a predator nearby. *Fuck.*

I didn't know what to do. If I ran, he would hear me. But if I stayed, he would scent me. I clenched my thighs, noting the dampness between my legs. Yeah, I was screwed. So, I would run.

I forced my body into action, but the moment I jumped out from behind the tree, a massive arm wrapped around my waist. I screamed and a rough clawed hand snapped out, covering my mouth and drowning the sound of my terror.

"Silly little doe. When a predator is hunting you, don't stop." Morax nipped at my ear, and I moaned. "Are you soaked for me, little doe? Your scent is intoxicating. You'll bring a whole horde of daemons down upon you with a delectable cunt like that."

The hand around my waist dipped lower until he cupped me fully between my legs. I whimpered as he pressed the heel of his hand on my clit. Morax turned us as one, walking us back to the massive tree.

He let go of me, and I turned back to speak, but before I could respond, he gripped my scalp tightly and forced me to face the tree instead. "Press your forearms against the tree and lean forward."

I didn't want to listen, I wanted to say something bratty. But my body had a mind of its own, and suddenly, I was pressing my arms to the tree, leaning at an angle and pushing my ass back toward him.

He chuckled again, running his claws down my back. "Good girl. I love it when you obey me."

My pussy throbbed at his words. I turned my head to the side and smiled at him. "Does that mean I get a reward?"

Morax grinned, and his daemon eyes glowed. His horns and wings were still out. I should have been terrified of this creature eyeing me like his next meal. But instead, my pussy was dripping with need and my mouth was dry as hell.

"You lost, little doe." He whipped his belt out from his jeans. "Before I take my reward, you will take five lashes from my belt for misbehaving earlier. And you will count them out."

Morax pushed my mesh dress up further then used his claws to tease my booty shorts down over my ass. He kept them just above my knees, so I couldn't move my legs. I gasped as the leather belt pressed between my legs, rubbing against my soaked core.

"When I pull this belt away, will it be dripping with your sweet juices, little doe?" Morax purred.

I moaned as he continued to rub the belt through my drenched lips.

"Even in the dark I can see your pretty pussy dripping for me."

He pulled the belt away, and a strangled sound left my

throat. I immediately missed the friction.

Morax laughed cruelly. "You're soaked for me, princess. Between the chase and the promise of my belt, you're nearly ready to come, aren't you?" He leaned in low, and his fangs tickled against ear. "Don't forget to count."

That was all the warning I had before the belt smacked against my ass.

I cried out, the sting bringing tears to my eyes. "One."

He brought the belt down again.

"Two."

And again.

"Three."

And again.

"Four."

My ass burned from the sting of each slap, and I could barely hold myself up against the tree. Even as I whimpered from the pain, I shuddered with desire for the beast causing it. His claws traced over my tender ass, making me shiver.

"One more, princess," Morax purred, his voice full of desire.

I felt powerful in this moment, a mere human causing this beast to lose control. "Do it."

The belt came down one final time, and I almost collapsed. My pussy was throbbing, aching for attention.

"Five."

Morax was on me in seconds. His hands rubbed softly over the tender spot on my ass. And then his tongue—oh, fucking gods, his forked tongue—slipped between my cheeks. His claws gently pulled my ass cheeks apart as he dropped to his knees behind me and licked from my ass to my soaked pussy. I didn't even recognize my voice from the sounds I was making. His tongue pressed between my lips and circled my clit. My body jerked forward, but he held me in place. He pulled away and kissed my ass oh so sweetly. The mix of gentle and rough touches made my head spin.

"Hold onto that tree, princess," Morax commanded.

I gripped the bark tightly, my body humming with excitement for what would come next. A desperate moan left my lips as he slipped one finger inside me, and he growled his approval.

"So fucking tight. My sweet little doe. Your pussy is gripping my finger so greedily. Do you want more?"

I gasped as he eased his finger in and out slowly. "Yes."

He chuckled and slid a second finger inside me. "That's my girl. So eager for me. I'm going to stretch this sweet cunt with my cock soon, princess. You were made for me. And I will never get enough of you."

Fireworks were starting to go off in my brain as his fingers fucked me harder and deeper. His tongue toyed with my ass as he expertly maneuvered his fingers to curl inside my pussy, making me see stars. His thumb rubbed a steady circle over my clit, and I screamed as the orgasm rushed through me. My legs gave out, but Morax caught me before I could fall. He laid me down on my back at the base of the tree and spread my legs wide, kneeling between them.

"You're going to give me one more, little doe," he demanded, his daemon eyes filled with lust.

Before I could respond, his mouth was on me again. He sucked my clit softly as he slid two fingers inside my pussy again. My back arched, and I moaned, overloaded with pleasure. My body was somehow working up to it again. I ground my pussy against his mouth and felt his grin between my thighs.

"Aren't we eager, princess? Are you going to be my slut tonight?" Morax murmured the words as he bit down on my thigh. "So eager for more of my fingers. My mouth."

I reached down and ran my fingers through his thick dark hair, pulling tight and trying to force his mouth down on me again. "More. Please."

Morax chuckled. "As you wish, princess."

My fingers gripped his hair tightly as he feasted on me with the desperation of a man at his last meal. His pinky gently nudged against my ass, and I gasped. He didn't stop. His tongue swirled my swollen clit, and his fingers fucked my pussy and my ass at a steady pace. I was going to lose my mind. The orgasm was building and building.

"Don't stop. Please don't stop." My hips bucked as he continued the assault. I screamed when my second orgasm shuddered through my body. He kept going, fucking me with his hand as I squirmed and cried out.

When he finally came up for air, Morax grinned a filthy smile, his lips and chin glistening with my cum. "I will never stop. You will never be rid of me, little lumen."

I couldn't respond. I had no thoughts, no breath, no strength. Morax gently slid my tiny shorts back on and scooped me up from the grass. He carried me, effortlessly, out of the woods and through the parking lot adjacent to the warehouse. The party was still raging inside, and no one noticed us. His horns and wings were gone, his claws retracted. Morax kissed my forehead and murmured sweet and dirty words as he carried me. He tucked me into the passenger seat of my Jeep and drove us back to my cabin. If he was worried about Father seeing him, Morax didn't show it. He carried me all the way to my room then stripped me out of my club clothes and into a soft T-shirt.

I didn't say much, didn't protest as he cared for me. The things I felt were so strange. My body was warm all the way through while he fussed over me. It felt fucking amazing having this deadly, beautiful monster taking such care of me.

When I was tucked into my bed, he kissed my forehead once more and exhaustion took over. I could barely keep my eyes open.

"Sleep well, princess." Morax whispered the words, and I think he said something else, but I was too far gone to hear them.

CHAPTER TEN

Michaela

The lazy morning sun pulled me from one of the best sleeps I'd had in years. I lay in bed, my eyes closed, playing out the scenes from last night in my mind. Morax brought out a side of me I'd never explored before. He made my body feel things and my lips say things I had only ever read in smutty novels. My body tingled at the memory of his tongue between my legs and my fingers tugging at his dark hair, silently begging him for more.

And I wanted more. Even now, my pussy throbbed and I knew if I slipped a finger or two down there, I would be soaked. Gods damn, I was falling hard for my daemon. And he was. *Mine.* He spoke the same words to me over and over. I was his. I belonged to him. And he was right. I was ruined for any future with some average human. My body submitted to him irrevocably. And my heart was following close behind.

I sat up quickly, needing a cold shower. Morax said something about killing that daemon, and he wasn't here now. Nervous energy made my anxiety grow. A part of me thought I would know if he were seriously injured. There were moments when I thought I could feel his emotions. The tiny scar where he cut my hand and our blood mingled would throb. I meant to ask him about the scar; I never had scars from injuries because of my ability to heal so quickly. I pressed my nail along the thin line and shivered when a jolt of electricity shot through me. He wasn't dead, I was sure of that.

After my shower, I slipped on a simple green summer dress and sneakers. I applied minimal makeup and quickly brushed the knots from my honey-colored hair. My father wasn't home, and we were also out of coffee, so I decided to go into town and grab myself an iced latte treat. I hopped on my bicycle, preferring to ride instead of walk. The summer sun beat down on my bare arms and legs as the wind whipped my hair. The exercise felt good, and the quiet ride helped calm my nerves.

The coffee shop wasn't packed, and I slipped through the line and found a table by the window to sip my iced hazelnut latte. I was only a few sips in when a stranger sat down in the chair across from me. He was around my age, with olive skin and dark hair. His deep-brown eyes were hollow. The lack of emotion instantly put me on edge.

"I need to deliver a message." His words were as unfeeling as his eyes. "It's about your family. Follow me. Now."

I didn't want to follow. It had to be a trap. And Morax wasn't here. But he mentioned my family. How could I not follow? I cursed inwardly at my lack of weapons. Why didn't I at least strap a blade to my thigh, damnit. My little blade was sitting on my nightstand, perfectly useless to me now.

"Morax, please come find me," I whispered as I followed the stranger out of the shop, hoping my daemon would hear me.

I stayed several paces back, giving myself enough space to bolt if I needed to. He was alone, though, and there were no strange cars lurking nearby. He wasn't particularly buff, so I had maybe an eighty percent chance of kicking his ass.

We walked briskly out of town, toward the woods I biked through to get to the cabin. I wondered for a moment if he knew where I lived, but he didn't go very far into the woods before stopping and turning toward me. I stopped as well, keeping a wary distance from him.

"Now tell me why I followed a stranger into the woods," I demanded, crossing my arms. "What do you know about my family?"

The stranger took a step forward, but before he could speak, a beast launched between us and pinned the guy to a tree by his throat. I smirked, realizing Morax must have heard my call.

"Who the fuck is this?" he growled, his eyes glowing that citrine yellow as his daemon form shimmered in and out of focus.

I shrugged. "I don't know yet. He says he has information about my family."

Morax turned to me, his eyes narrowed as his gaze traced my body from head to toe. "So you followed a stranger, alone and without weapons, into the middle of the woods? Little lumen, I might have to strangle you when I'm done with him."

He emphasized the words by squeezing the stranger's throat. The guy's feet kicked several inches above the ground as his hands clawed uselessly at the muscular arm holding him in place.

I grinned, and Morax raised an eyebrow at me. "I called you, didn't I? You're my best and preferred weapon of choice."

Morax huffed, a low growl vibrating through my bones, and his eyes dilated. How was I so turned on already?

"Can you not kill him yet? I want to hear what he has to say." I stepped closer to them and placed my hand on his extended arm.

Morax dropped the guy to the ground.

He coughed and choked, sucking down fresh oxygen.

"I've already read his thoughts. He knows very little. But he has something for you." Morax kept his body partially in front of mine, shielding me from the stranger. "Give her the device."

It was my turn to arch an eyebrow. The stranger stood slowly and pulled a small handheld video camera from his pocket. "In the event of his death, I was told to deliver this message."

Morax grabbed the camera from the guy before I could reach for it and handed it to me instead. Overprotective, psycho daemon.

I popped out the small screen and turned it on. There was one video on the camera, and I pressed play with shaking fingers. A man appeared, and not one I knew.

Hello, Michaela. If you are watching this, death has come for me. My name is Ezekiel Parrish, and I am one of the four Obscuritas Kings.

My hands shook, but not from fear. This was one of the men who murdered Lailah and our mother.

I am not proud of my actions. And I know at this time my words mean very little to you. But we have very little time left, so you must listen. I met your mother many years ago. After my wife and child were murdered, your mother came to me. Unlike the other Kings, I loved my wife and my children. I was desperate to get them back and would have done anything to make that happen. It was not meant to be, but I could change what would come next and still save my son. Devon Parrish is an Obscuritas Prince, and he will need your help.

Fat fucking chance of that. The mention of my mother meeting with this asshole had my mind reeling. Every little bit of information I gained about my mother only made me angrier. She was this great seer, and she knew so much, but she still died. Still let Lailah die.

Your mother showed me what would come next. The darkness that would take over our world and her own world. If we carried on this path, no one would survive. There was only a small window of opportunity to make things right. You and your sisters are that opportunity. Take the gift. I have kept it these many years for you and Seraphina. The other Kings will come for you soon. Let them take you.

Morax growled so loud I jumped. Heat radiated from his body as he cursed at the camera.

You must do this and remain strong. Use the daemon to find your sister. Help her friend, as her mind will be lost. The rituals must happen. Kill the messenger. When you see my son, tell him I am sorry. Tell him I loved him.

The video ended, and I stared at the sad, dark eyes of the man in the camera. I believed him. His desperation was evident, and the unending sadness in his eyes was real.

"For you. And for your sister." The stranger pulled out two small boxes.

Morax took them first and handed me the one with a golden M engraved on it. I opened the box and found a delicate necklace with a strange stone wrapped in gold. It looked similar to an opal.

Morax sucked in a breath, and I turned to him.

"That stone is called luxenite. It is, essentially, the essence of a lumen. When a lumen dies, they can choose to turn their soul, their essence, into a gift for another. It can be used only once. And each one is different. The power that comes from the stone varies based on the lumen who provided it. Most lumens do not do this." His voice was in awe as he stared at the necklace.

I turned to him, curious. "Why not?"

Morax frowned. "When we do eventually die, it is not like a human death. We let go of our earthly form and ascend to the stars to watch over all those still living. When a lumen creates the luxenite, they forfeit their place among the stars. Daemons have something similar, and it is even rarer. It is called tenebrite."

We looked down at the box engraved with an S. Morax opened it slowly and gasped once more. The stone was deepest blue with flecks of back, like a sapphire mixed with onyx.

"Is that tenebrite?" I asked, my voice near a whisper.

Morax nodded.

"Who were they? Can you tell?" I needed to know who would give us such gifts.

He shook his head. "I do not know. I will try to find out. These are rare gifts indeed." He closed the box for my sister and handed it to me as I closed mine.

The wind whipped my hair as Morax turned and, without blinking, tore his claws into the stranger's chest and ripped out his heart. The body dropped to the ground, and I stood, mouth open and in shock. Morax took the video camera from my hand and proceeded to crush it into dust with his sharp claws.

"What the hell just happened?" I shouted at him, coming out of my shocked silence. The air smelled like iron, so strong I could almost taste it.

"The Obscuritas King said it first, and he was right. Kill the messenger." Morax turned to the body and whispered a few words under his breath.

The dead messenger suddenly caught fire and disintegrated in minutes.

"He had to die, little lumen."

CHAPTER ELEVEN

Morax

Michaela was quiet as we walked back to the cabin. I used a bit of my magic to pull her bike along with us. She wanted to go for a long ride alone, but I refused to leave her side. Gremory escaped, and I wasn't sure how this would play out. He was more cunning than I expected, masking his scent and his power, even with the injuries he sustained during our fight. The last thing I wanted to do was frighten my mate, but she had to know the danger of the situation. Once again, she surprised me with her courage. She listened to my recount of the night after I dropped her safely at the cabin and went on the hunt. I suspected The Obscuritas would come for her and her father. It would be foolish to think Gremory did not sense her, since we did not know exactly why he was at the warehouse party in the first place. It was even more troubling that the now-dead lumen hybrid was working with him. The Obscuritas had more power than I realized, with allies from my world working for them.

The dead Obscuritas King offering his help was a pleasant surprise. Well, not entirely a surprise. My gossiping younger brother, Phenex, mentioned something about allies on the inside. He was terrible at keeping secrets, but so far only slipped a few details of his master plan to me. I wasn't being fully transparent with Michaela either. Phen and I knew her mother a bit more than I let on. We met her several times, and Lailah once. As Aurora was lumen royalty, we met when my brothers and I were very young. Lailah was a newborn, and all royal babies were to be presented to the other royals. It was the way of things before war between our kinds ended any kind of peace.

I knew something disturbed her even then, because we never saw her or her daughter again. Word came of her lumen husband's death not long after Lailah's second birthday. The true shock was the discovery of Aurora's daemon lover many years later. How she was able to hide so many things from so many prying eyes was still a mystery. I never met the daemon, Seraphina's father. But Phenex did meet him, just before the daemon was killed. My brother was silent for many weeks, which was incredibly strange. He would not tell me what happened that day, what the daemon said to him.

But since then, many things had come to pass, according to Phenex, that he was told would happen. I had an inkling he knew I would end up mated to the little lumen walking beside me. And I would most definitely be kicking his ass for allowing me to be blindsided with the knowledge.

Michaela was humming a song under her breath, the sound like a lullaby to my heightened hearing. Her beautiful blue and hazel eyes stared ahead, unseeing as she was deep in thought. While I couldn't hear her thoughts, I could sense her troubled emotions, and the desire to soothe her became too strong. I grabbed her arm and stopped her, pulling her close as I wrapped my arms around her slim waist. She looked positively edible in her little sundress and sneakers. Her blonde hair caught the sunlight in a way that perfectly highlighted the many shades of her natural balayage. I was constantly mesmerized by her beauty and her inability to see herself as I did.

"Tell me what you're thinking, little lumen." I spoke with authority, urging her to obey me. Her distress caused a need in me to destroy whatever it was that made her so.

Michaela turned her head up to look at me, giving me a full view of this pretty creature who would be mine for eternity.

Her eyes dipped to my lips, and I smirked as her scent changed to something more depraved. She blushed, knowing I could sense it.

"Well, I was mulling over everything Ezekiel said. And I just wish I knew more about my mother." Michaela sighed. "I wish she could've left me something, even videos like that, so I could understand all of this. Every time I learn something new, it's like I'm starting over again. Why can't people leave clear and specific instructions on how to do things?"

I started to respond, but she interrupted, apparently building up for a good rant. She tried to pull away, but I held her in place, locked safely in my arms.

"You know? Like a nice long letter that says, *Hello daughters, let me tell you all the crazy shit that happened before I brought you into this world. And all the crazy shit you will have to deal with after I get murdered.*" Michael huffed irritably. "If she was such a brilliant seer, why is she dead? Why is Lailah dead?"

I leaned forward and rested my forehead against hers. "Being a great seer is more of a burden, or a curse, than an advantage. Perhaps she saw things, to the very end, and this path was the only one leading to a positive outcome."

Michaela closed her eyes, and I could feel the sadness deepen within her. "What outcome is positive enough to warrant their deaths? I would give anything to have my family back together again."

Her sadness was breaking my heart, and there was little I could do to rid her of it. I slipped my hand beneath her chin, and she looked up at me with watery eyes. "I can only imagine the future she must have seen for her to choose this path. I did not know your mother well, but I have heard she loved her daughters more fiercely than a lioness. The future she saw must have been dark indeed for her to choose this path for her children. But she knew you would be strong enough to do what must be done."

"I don't even know what that is. What am I supposed to do?" she whispered softly.

I kissed her forehead, willing a sense of calm over her. "I don't have all the answers, little lumen. But I do believe the fates of our worlds are connected. And we will both play a part in saving them."

Michaela rolled her eyes. "Sounds terrible."

I chuckled at the grumpy tone of her voice. "I am grateful for your mother's actions and her sacrifices. They brought me to you. That is something I will never be sorry for."

My mate blushed, and her eyes dilated as she stared up at me, seeing the truth of my words. I wanted so badly to tell her we were fated by the stars to be together, but I was also terrified of her reaction. Growing up on Earth, such things didn't exist. I could feel her desire for me, but while her lumen side was locked down, she couldn't truly feel the mating bond.

So instead of pouring my bleeding heart out for her, I kissed her softly, nipped her lip possessively, and turned us back toward the cabin.

We were nearly there, only one turn through the woods before the cabin would be visible, when the air shifted. I growled, my wings snapping out and my horns protruding from the crown of my head. I turned so my body blocked Michaela's.

"What is it?" she whispered, grabbing my arm.

"They're here. The Obscuritas are in the cabin with your father. They have come to take you both."

The thought of that filthy cult taking my mate had a growl building deep in my chest. I couldn't sense any other daemons or lumens present. They sent humans, and I could easily kill them all.

Michaela squeezed my arm. "We knew this would happen."

I snarled, my fangs descending, but my mate did not back away.

She grabbed my face, pulling me close. "Go back to the police station. Figure out how to join the security detail and come find me. I'll be okay until then."

My skin felt hot at the thought of leaving her, leaving her with them.

"Keep these safe for me." She slipped the two small jewelry boxes into the back pocket of my jeans.

Michaela's delicate hands reached up and stroked my horns, making me shiver with pleasure. If anyone else had attempted to touch my horns, I'd rip out their throat. But not her. Never her.

"I don't know if I can do it. I don't want to leave you with those monsters."

Her hands slid down my jawline, and her thumb brushed across my lips. "I can handle the humans for a bit."

My tongue snaked out to taste her, and she smiled.

"I'll be bringing the real monster to them. And when the time comes, I'll unleash my daemon on every one of those fuckers."

My cock twitched at her filthy little mouth. "Unleash me, princess? I didn't realize you'd collared me."

Michaela twined her arms around my neck and jumped up. I caught her thighs as she wrapped her legs around my waist.

"That's because I'm sneaky."

I chuckled and burrowed my nose against her neck, inhaling her sweet scent. I could eat her up. Her pulse quickened as I moved closer to her ear, licking and sucking her pretty skin.

"Every single one of them who dares touch what is mine will lose a limb. Or their life. Remember their names, princess. And when I come for you, tell me the names of the pathetic humans who dared to harm my mate."

The word slipped out, and there was nothing I could do to take it back. Michaela's breath hitched, but before she could speak, a helicopter flew overhead, stealing her attention. We were out of time.

CHAPTER TWELVE

Michaela

Mate. He called me his mate.

And I was pretty sure he didn't mean it like we were best buds. No. He was claiming me, or had claimed me, in some primal way that I wasn't even aware existed. My brain was short-circuiting with this information, but I had no time to dwell on it. The blacked-out helicopter soared over the woods and toward my home. The Obscuritas were here to take me. What would happen next, I had no idea. But I had to trust my mother knew what she was doing when she set us all down this road.

I slipped out of Morax's arms, unable to look him in the eye, and turned in the direction of the cabin. He grabbed my hand and yanked me back, forcing me to look at him, his daemon eyes glowing with emotion.

"I will be with you again soon. Don't do anything reckless until I arrive. Understood?" His voice was rough and demanding.

Part of me wanted to clap back with something sassy, but the tinge of desperation in his eyes held me back. My daemon—my mate—would literally burn everything to hell if I was hurt. And we weren't ready for that.

So instead, I nodded. "I'll behave. For now." I squeezed his hand. "Come soon, though, okay?"

I could pretend to be brave all I wanted, but these were still the people who murdered my mother and sister. They *were* dangerous, and I would never forget that.

Morax pulled me in close and kissed me. It was a hard, probing kiss. I opened up to him, and his forked tongue devoured mine. He tugged my hair hard and wrapped his other hand around my throat, owning me fully with this kiss. Something inside me lit up, and my blood began to sing. I could feel a power deep within me stirring. I gasped, and he pulled away.

His eyes captured mine, staring at me with lust and adoration. It felt like my body was catching fire from within, and I could almost feel the emotions rolling off my daemon as the power pulsed inside me.

"You are so fucking beautiful, little lumen. Brave. Clever. Fierce." Morax kissed me between each word. "And you have the most decadent pussy I've ever tasted."

I moaned as he kissed me again, and my skin felt like it was glowing. He pulled away, letting go of me, and it was as if a cloud passed in front of the sun. I missed his touch already.

"Now go. I'll see you soon." Morax passed my bike to me.

I climbed on and pedaled away without looking back. If I looked back, I wouldn't be able to leave him.

The woods thinned, and the cabin came into view, surrounded by three SUVs and a fucking helicopter. You'd think we were superstars. Or supervillains. Either way, this seemed like overkill. The men standing on the front porch drew their guns as I pedaled closer.

"Stop right there!" one of them yelled at me. "Get off the bike and walk toward us with your hands in front, where we can see them."

I rolled my eyes but did as they asked. I promised Morax I would behave. And I needed to see that my father was unharmed.

When I reached the porch, the one who yelled stepped forward and immediately cuffed my hands behind my back.

"What's your name, dumbass?" I asked, smiling.

He tightened the cuffs, and I winced. He seemed to like that. "Tony."

I stared him dead in the eyes. "Looking forward to your dismemberment, Tony."

The dumbass laughed, but his eyes showed fear. My daemon would have fun with this one.

The three men marched me into the house. My father was seated at the kitchen table, his hands cuffed in his lap. Four more men stood around him. A fifth man in a navy suit walked out of my room, brushing invisible lint from his sleeve. Other than his very expensive clothing, he was incredibly dull. His dark-brown hair was laced with silver, and his shit-brown eyes narrowed at me as he walked down the hall and into the room.

"Michaela, I presume?" His monotone voice suited the overall lame persona. "I am Professor Lehmann. You may call me sir."

I snorted a laugh and rolled my eyes. "Not likely."

Soldier boy Tony pushed me from behind, and I fell hard to my knees. My father started to protest, but another soldier shoved him back down into his chair.

I looked back at Tony, grinding my teeth. "Just keep digging your grave then."

The professor cleared his throat and stepped closer. He grabbed my face, and I used all of my self-control not to struggle as his slimy hands touched me. "It's a shame I can't punish you now. But the Kings want you. I do hope I get the chance to play with you once they're finished, though. The pretty thing I have locked in the basement won't last much longer."

Fiery rage built inside me at his words. I wished Morax was here to rip apart this disgusting pig. He was now number one on my list of names. As soon as my daemon returned, we'd do something about this piece of shit.

Professor Lehmann smacked my face, not enough to bruise, but enough to sting. He was testing my reactions. This fucker liked to see his victims cower before him. Well, that would not be me. I stared up at him with hate and defiance. His dull face twitched with unease. The scrawny professor looked away first. I was right, he did not like strong women.

"It's time to go." He walked to the front door, turning back to the soldiers. "Get them to the Kings. I have a sub I need to punish."

"You piece of shit!" I screamed, struggling against the handcuffs. He was going back to

hurt that girl because of me. I pissed him off, and now some poor girl was going to pay for it.

Professor Lehmann smirked at me before leaving the house. I heard the helicopter, the sound fading away with the man I needed my daemon to kill. He wouldn't get there in time to save her from her next round of torture, and that ate me up inside.

The soldiers guided us to the blacked-out SUVs. They also

loaded several cases and our safe into a third SUV. I assumed our house was raided and they found my mother's things. Her books were secure for now. I changed the code on the safe only yesterday, not even my father knew it.

I climbed awkwardly into the back of the SUV. Tony climbed into the front passenger seat, and another man got into the driver's seat. The others loaded into the SUV with my father.

"Where are we going?" I asked, not expecting an answer.

Tony turned his head slightly and smirked. "Your home for the foreseeable future, just outside of Charlotte, North Carolina."

Cold dread seeped through my skin at his words. I knew where we were going. The last time I was there, my mother and sister were murdered. This day was coming, I knew that. But I couldn't help the feelings of nausea and terror as I remembered my last night at The Obscuritas Mansion. Even with the drugs my father had given me to knock me out, I could still hear their screams. I would always hear their screams.

Now was not the time for fear, though. I had about four hours to collect myself before we arrived. Closing my eyes, I centered my mind and relaxed my breathing until I felt a semblance of calm. I sent my thoughts away to my daemon, begging him to find me soon.

The drive was excruciating. I used the time to think of all the ways my daemon would kill these men. Sometimes when my thoughts lingered on him, it almost felt like he was there. My palm would tingle where he cut it and licked my blood, and emotions that didn't feel entirely my own filled my mind. I needed to ask him about that little ritual. I think sharing blood with a daemon was more than just some pact. And that other thing. Mate. Could I feel him because he was my mate? How did that work? I had so many fucking questions and no damn time to ask them.

When we finally pulled through a set of iron gates, my anxiety spiked. I remembered this drive. The lane was dominated by tall trees. Massive statues of daemons and creatures I didn't recognize lined the drive as we got nearer to the house.

"Welcome home," Tony snickered.

"Enjoy it while it lasts, asshole."

He frowned at me, and I ignored him. Dead men weren't worth my time. The SUVs pulled up directly in front of the house. Grand stone steps lead to double doors made of wood and iron. My father turned to me as soon as he was out of the first SUV. I gave him a grim, and hopefully reassuring, smile. He didn't smile back. He rarely smiled. But he nodded, his salt and pepper hair falling across his eyes.

They walked us into the mansion. Everything here was over the top. The ceilings were no less than thirty feet high, and huge portraits of lame old men lined the walls, painted in shades of black and gray. Heavy velvet curtains lined every window, letting in very little light. The hallway opened to a large sitting room, decorated in similar dark and moody colors. Candles and dim sconces provided the only light.

Sitting on two of the couches were two men I never wanted to see again. I knew their faces, studied them and tracked them however I could. The first one was slightly shorter, maybe 5'10", with light-brown hair perfectly styled. He had an easy smile that would charm most women, but immediately made me want to puke. He wore navy slacks and a white button-down shirt with the sleeves rolled up. His left ankle was propped on his right knee, and he stroked the glass of bourbon in his hand as he smiled at me. Samuel Delano. Blue eyes winked at me, and I turned away before I said something that would get me in trouble. I promised my daemon I would behave.

Sitting across from him, his massive forearms resting on his equally massive thighs, was Darren Radnor. He was dressed more casually, a fitted T-shirt showing off tattoos and scars. Everything about him set alarm bells ringing in my brain. My body physically recoiled as he stared at me, his dark eyes moving down my body. He licked his lips, and the grin on his face was pure evil. I hated him the most. Morax would need to kill this one soon. But even as sadistic Darren Radnor was, he was nothing compared to the evil lurking in the final Obscuritas King.

Laszlo Blackbyrn walked into the room, his eyes assessing my father before landing on me. He was the unequivocal leader of the Kings. They were all Obscuritas Kings, but Laszlo's decisions for the cult were always final and unchallenged. His hair was trimmed short, and he wore a tailored, dark-green suit. His light-green eyes were startling against his dark skin. If he weren't so totally evil, he could be beautiful. Laszlo stopped in front of me, and I saw my father attempt to step closer, but a guard pulled him back.

"This is a very good day." Laszlo's voice was deep. He smiled, but it didn't reach his eyes.

I fought the urge to shiver as he moved closer. I couldn't step back without pressing against dumbass Tony, so I held my ground and stared up at Laszlo.

"I would welcome you with a tour, but perhaps you remember it?" Laszlo's arm reached out, and he tugged my hair between his fingers. "So much like your mother's. You resemble her even more than Lailah did."

Welp, that was it. I snapped my teeth at his hand, but he pulled away too quickly. "Don't fucking talk about them."

Laszlo smirked. "She's going to be a fun toy for you, Darren."

An ominous chuckle came from the far couch, and Darren rose from his seat. He looked terrifying. His smile was wicked, and his eyes burned into my flesh. Bile rose in my throat as he came toward me. His hand wrapped around my throat, and I couldn't help the gasp that escaped my lips. Darren's fingers dug into my skin, and I began to see spots as my oxygen was cut off.

He pulled me close, our faces nearly touching. "Oh, yes. I'm going to enjoy playing with you. I didn't get to fuck your pretty lumen sister like I wanted. Everything happened so fast. But this time, I'll take my time."

I needed oxygen desperately. His massive hands squeezed, and I was so close to passing out. His words were like knives digging under my skin. I would throw myself out a window before I let him touch me.

"Best not kill her then, Radnor," Samuel called from the couch, sipping his drink.

Darren let go of my throat, and I wheezed. My knees buckled, and the only thing keeping me from falling was Tony's grip on my wrists, which were still cuffed behind my back.

My throat burned and my vision was still blurring as I sucked down gulps of air.

"You," I whispered, struggling to get the words out. I coughed twice and forced my back to straighten.

Darren was smiling, clearly enjoying my pain. I smiled back at him. My own grin grew as his faded.

"I'm going to enjoy watching you die."

Lazlo smirked at me before he turned to Darren. "Take her to her room. We will be hosting dinner for our guests this evening."

They left me alone in a massive bedroom. Everything in this stupid mansion was over-decorated in the most dramatic fashion. The dark and moody vibes continued, with thick, purple velvet curtains blotting out the light. The four-poster bed was shrouded in sheer curtains, and the walls held sconces with flickering candles. I walked to the two doors on the opposite wall. The first was a walk-in closet outfitted with dozens of dresses, shoes, and jewelry. If I wasn't being held captive by dick heads, this would be so awesome. The second door led to a beautiful bathroom complete with a clawfoot tub big enough for two people.

I wandered back into the room and stopped short when I saw a man standing by the bed. His hand brushed over the wooden posts lazily as he turned to me. The look in his eyes had my own darting to the door.

"Do you like your accommodations, Michaela?" Darren

Radnor's voice was poisonous. The sound of it made my skin crawl. "You know, this doesn't have to be a prison."

My eyes widened. Could he read my thoughts? I was just thinking that very word.

Darren chuckled. "I can read some of your thoughts. Your powerful blood keeps us out, but you wear your emotions on your face. And when I startled you just now, I snuck in."

He walked toward me, and I held my shoulders straight, my back rigid. I would not show him fear. I could not let him get inside my head. The fact that he did made me feel violated. I wanted to vomit.

Darren was a massive man. Not as big as my daemon, but muscular enough his shadow swallowed up my own. His fingers traced along my collarbone, and I fought the urge to shiver with disgust.

"The other Kings are giving me a prize for all I've done to make this come to pass. I wanted the youngest one. The innocent one. But tell me, Michaela, are you still?"

I swallowed as his hand traced down my side and across my belly. "Still what?"

His eyes were glued to my chest as I tried to keep my breathing even. "A virgin."

My skin felt hot all over as the blush creeped up my neck. He grinned as his eyes returned to my face. The violence in them was horrific, and I couldn't help trying to run. He grabbed me by the throat and held me still before I could move so much as an inch.

"I am so glad to hear it. One way or another, I will have your submission, Michaela. I cannot wait to feel your innocent body writhing beneath me. To ruin this sweet cunt."

Darren's other hand cupped my pussy over my shorts, and I wanted to melt into the floor. I couldn't form any words. My mind and body were shutting down even as I screamed internally. This was happening too fast, too soon.

CHAPTER THIRTEEN
Morax

I felt her fear and was seconds from losing my shit when it subsided. Not fully, but enough. I used every ounce of willpower I had to stay in my human form. We were driving to the mansion and about ten minutes away. I was seated in the front passenger seat. The other guards chatted amicably on the drive from the police station. There were an annoying amount of humans working for this fucking cult. They were handpicked by Darren Radnor for extra security now that their "guests" had arrived. It was easy to blur their memories and force my existence into their minds. Now I was just another guard, and the captain chose me specifically to guard the young female prisoner. I would need to adjust Darren Radnor's mind some as well, which would be more difficult. The Kings were drawing on daemonic power, but they weren't strong enough to shut me out completely. I was mostly certain of that.

Just as we arrived at the mansion, Michaela's fear spiked again, and my nostrils flared. I growled, and the guard driving glanced my way curiously. I couldn't speak as I felt her mind screaming for my help. We parked in a small lot behind the mansion and walked toward a rear entrance. If I didn't find her soon, I was going to blow my cover and burn this entire building to the ground.

The guards walked swiftly through the mansion, and the captain stopped at a set of stairs.

He turned to me. "The female should be in her bedroom, up these stairs and the second door on the left. Go to the door and stand guard until I radio with further instructions. She does not leave that room unless requested by the Kings."

I nodded and immediately took to the stairs. I didn't need to hear what other orders were given; I needed to find my fucking mate. The moment I reached the top of the stairs, I could smell her. She was terrified. When I finally reached the door and ripped it open, I saw why she was so scared.

Darren Radnor was holding her by the throat, his other hand between her legs. It took every bit of my power not to transform and rip off his head. I straightened slowly as Darren turned my way.

"Sir. The Kings are looking for you." My voice was steady as I spoke.

Michaela's eyes were wide with relief and boring into mine.

Darren turned back to her, giving her throat a squeeze. "Wear something nice for me, sweet girl."

He let go of her, looking satisfied. I wanted to fight him. Even in human form, he was smaller than I was. But I wanted to unleash my daemon and torture him slowly for touching my fucking mate.

"Make sure she gets cleaned up for dinner and brought downstairs shortly," he growled at me, thinking I would cower like any other guard. And I did, I fucking did so our plan would stay intact.

He left the room, and I closed the door, turning back to Michaela. I was by her side in two massive strides. My horns and claws slipped out and my skin glowed red as I lost control. I pulled her into my arms and buried my face in her hair, scenting her, comforting her. She whimpered, her body molding to mine.

I pulled back and cupped her face with my hands, careful of my claws. "Did he hurt you?"

She shook her head. "He was trying to scare me. It worked."

My heart broke at her words. I should've come sooner. I was failing her. "I will kill him. Slowly. He will beg for mercy as I cut each limb from his body and lay them at your feet."

Michaela huffed a laugh. "I'm going to hold you to that someday. For now, maybe just figure out a way to keep him from raping me."

I snarled, and power radiated out of me. I could feel my eyes glowing. "He will never get the chance. Never."

Michaela's hands slid up to my face. She did not shy away from my daemon form. Her mismatched eyes searched mine, and her lips pressed into a thin line. "I know. We will stop him. I trust you, Morax."

I brought my lips down to hers and kissed her roughly, urging her to let me in. She opened for me like a flower, and I drove my tongue between her plump lips, teasing the roof of her mouth with my forked tongue. She moaned, leaning into me, her soft hands threading my hair. A deep purr built in my chest as she attempted to reach higher, her fingers brushing against the base of my horns. Her touch set me on fire. Horns and wings were off limits to anyone but your mate.

I slipped a hand into her blonde hair and gripped at the

base of her head, pulling her back enough to break our kiss. A possessive growl escaped me, and her eyes dilated. "As much as I want to continue this, we need to get you dressed for dinner. They need to believe in your submission. For now."

Michaela nodded, and her shoulders slumped. She turned away from me, attempting to escape, but I wasn't ready to let her go.

I tightened my hold on her hair and tilted her head back, forcing her to look at me. My pretty mate. "I will be by your side every moment until we end this."

"Unfortunately, it's only the beginning," she murmured, and I nodded, because it was true. And I had no idea if we could pull this off.

Michaela's slender arm was threaded through mine as we walked the halls of the massive home. She chose a navy satin dress with thin straps tied behind her neck. The fabric was thin enough I could see her peaked nipples through the material. My mouth watered, and I growled possessively. I reached toward the left one and pinched it. She yelped and grinned.

She smacked my chest. "What was that for?"

"For allowing these filthy fuckers to see so much of you," I snarled, hating this plan of hers. "I'm going to tear their eyes from their skulls for staring at my mate's perfect, peaked nipples."

Michaela giggled. I wanted to kiss her and swallow the sound. Her happiness was everything to me and I craved it constantly.

"You know it's a good plan." She looked up at me as we walked, the soft fabric of her long dress swaying at her feet. Even in heels, she was so much smaller than me.

My brave little lumen. I gritted my teeth, because she was right. Having her dressed so exquisitely would drive Darren Radnor wild. And with his attention so focused on her, I could slip into his mind.

When we finally made our way into the dining room, I reluctantly released her arm and walked behind her instead. I would be in deep shit if the Kings saw a guard touching her. The Kings were not in the room, but we were not the first to arrive. A petite girl with short, pink hair sat at the table. Her eyes were glazed over as she sat with her back straight, unmoving.

Michaela continued to walk closer to the girl, and I hissed behind her. Just because the female looked small and unarmed didn't mean she wasn't dangerous. I tried to slip into her mind, but it was muddied with darkness. Someone was already toying with this human.

"Hello," Michaela spoke cautiously to the female.

The pink-haired human blinked twice and turned her face to my mate's. She didn't smile. "Hello."

I pulled out the chair next to the female, and Michaela sat down beside her. "I'm Michaela. Who are you?"

"Tabitha. Tibby is fine too," the female spoke softly and looked around, her eyes darting around the room. "We shouldn't be talking."

I scanned the female further and noticed bruises peaking around her clothes. She wore a short black dress, if you could call it that. It barely covered her too-thin body. A cruel collar with spikes facing inward was wrapped tightly around her neck, not enough to make her bleed, but enough to make her hurt any time she spoke.

"She is right, princess," I murmured, tuning my ears for the sound of footsteps. We were alone for now. I scanned the room and noted cameras hidden throughout, similar to the hallways. As far as I could tell, only bedrooms and bathrooms were free of the hidden cameras.

Michaela reached out and gently took Tabitha's hand into her own. "Who did this to you?"

Tibby's bottom lip quivered, and tears threatened to spill over. "I didn't want to, but I couldn't stop. I can't stop. They're inside my mind."

Michaela glanced up at me, and I nodded, probing the female's mind again. A face appeared with features similar to my mate's. "She knows your sister."

"Tibby, where is my sister?" Michaela whispered harshly.

Tibby shook her head. "She is not here. Not yet. They have plans. I can't say." Tibby grabbed her head suddenly and winced. "I can't say."

I pressed my hand to Michaela's back. "Her mind is not her own anymore."

My beautiful mate turned to me, her eyes desperate. "Can you help her? Maybe you can find Seraphina first. She must be the friend Ezekiel mentioned."

When the tortured female spoke, I instantly thought of the video message. Michaela was correct. This human's mind was lost, but I could try to mend it. She might have knowledge locked away that could help us.

Before I could speak, footsteps caught my attention. "The Kings are coming."

Tibby's eyes widened, and she quickly jumped from her seat. She walked several paces back from the table and dropped into a kneeling position, her face pressed to the floor in supplication. I frowned, but there was no time to question her. I stepped behind Michaela's chair where she remained seated. The Kings entered the room, and I resisted the urge to roll my eyes. To other humans, these men appeared confident and terrifying, but I could smell their fears. Their insecurities. And their mind-altering desires for power. I could not fully read their thoughts. The dark-skinned one at the center, Laszlo Blackbyrn, was particularly difficult to read. His expression was bored as his eyes trailed to Tibby. He smirked, and a sliver of pleasure slipped through before he collected himself. This one was responsible for the female's scrambled mind.

Darren Radnor stalked toward the table, eyeing Michaela like a piece of meat. His lust was flooding my nostrils, and I soothed my daemon form as much as possible.

"Well, well. I see you're already obeying my orders. You look delicious." His voice was rough with desire as he pushed me aside and placed his hands on my mate's throat from behind. "Next time, you will kneel beside Tabitha and wait for me in that position. Understood?"

Michaela's mouth flattened, and her eyes darted toward me, filled with anger. She took a breath and nodded. Darren grinned and reached down the front of her dresses and palmed her breast. She didn't move.

I snarled, and the attention of three Kings snapped my

way. I recovered quickly, coughing like something was stuck in my throat. When I straightened, my face remained blank and I stared at the floor.

The Kings returned their attention to the table, taking their seats. A few moments later, another group of guards brought in Michaela's father. He was dressed in a suit and sporting a bruised face. His eyes zeroed in on Darren groping my mate, and he started to shout.

"Not a word, Joseph," Darren snapped. "I'm playing nice. If you behave, I will continue to play nice."

Joseph's face was furious, but his lips remained closed. We were both locked in our positions and unable to do anything. The only fucking benefit to this bullshit was Darren's shields were weakening with Michaela distracting him. I slipped through the shield and read his thoughts.

That was a mistake. My skin started to glow as I felt his desire to rape and mutilate my mate. I could feel my wings itching to snap out and the tips of my horns poked through my hair. I closed my eyes and forced my breathing to slow, focusing on Michaela and the strength she had to remain calm while this vile fucking human touched her. If she could do that, I could do this for her.

I sifted through his thoughts as the Kings chatted about nothing interesting and Joseph proceeded to sit at the table. Darren finally let go of my little lumen and seated himself next to her. Servants entered the room with trays of food.

"Laszlo, will your little pet be joining us for dinner?" Samuel Delano finally spoke. His expression was mildly amused. He was smaller than Laszlo and Darren, but no less dangerous.

This one had a dark mind. I could feel it even through his mental shields.

Laszlo turned to Tibby. "Come here, slave."

Tibby slowly stood, keeping her eyes down as she walked to Laszlo. She dropped to her knees again, her hands splayed on her thighs.

Laszlo picked up a piece of bread and tore a piece with his teeth, chewing slowly before turning to Tibby. He grabbed her chin and forced her mouth open. Laszlo spit the chewed up bread into Tibby's mouth. "Swallow."

I could see from here the tears burning in the human's eyes, but she obeyed. Tibby chewed and swallowed the bread. "Thank you, master."

Darren laughed loudly and wrapped his hand around Michaela's throat. "I cannot wait to hear you call me master when I fuck that virgin pussy."

Michaela remained silent, her body rigid as she forced herself not to react. My beautiful, strong mate. Radnor wanted her fear, her reactions to his touch, and she refused to give in. I sent strength and fierceness to her, pressing my power against her mind like a warm embrace. Her heart rate slowed, and mine followed.

Samuel chuckled. "She's going to be a tough one to break, Darren. I bet she would last long strapped to my table as well. Perhaps I'll lend you some of my toys."

Darren smacked Michaela's cheek lightly, and I grimaced. "Yes, she needs to be broken in properly."

Laszlo's eyes snapped to Darren angrily. "Not yet. Leave her somewhat whole for now, Darren. We need her to be of sound mind to get her sister's cooperation."

Darren rolled his eyes, and Samuel slumped slightly in his chair.

"I know the fucking rules. Once we have Seraphina under control, we can play." Darren gripped Michaela's cheeks tightly, turning her face to his. "Until then, you'll be a very good girl for me, won't you?"

Michaela remained silent, and his grip tightened. A slight whimper escaped her lips from the pain, and I stepped toward her. Laszlo noted my movement, and I stopped, looking down.

"Won't you?" Darren growled at my mate.

"Yes." She whispered the word, and he let go of her once more. Her jaw ticked with anger, mirroring my own.

Laszlo was watching now. I needed to be more careful. I could feel his power slithering against my mental shields. I would have to let him in a little or he would grow suspicious. I created a set of false memories and pushed them to the front of my mind. All he would see was me, excited to serve these Kings and hoping for power in return for my loyalty. Laszlo's power slipped away, satisfied, and he continued to eat, occasionally spitting food into Tibby's mouth and forcing her to swallow it.

These fucking Kings deserved fates worse than death. And it would be my absolute fucking pleasure to deal out those fates.

CHAPTER FOURTEEN
Michaela

Dinner with the Kings was the worst fucking thing ever. I knew being their prisoner would be difficult, but bile rose from the pit of my stomach the moment Darren Radnor's hand squeezed my breast. Only Morax and his soothing strength kept me still as the leech assaulted me. Watching Tibby willingly eat Laszlo's chewed up food was almost worse. I could see the bruises on her skin. And that spiked collar…I couldn't imagine the things Laszlo Blackbyrn was doing to her in private if this was what he did to her in front of others.

Morax and I walked silently back to my room. I felt eyes on us every step of the way. I didn't speak to my father. How could I, when he had witnessed my assault? Truthfully, his submission hurt more than anything. I just wanted him to fight for us, fight for something. Sure, dumbass Darren threatened to do worse, but still. A girl can be a little heartbroken when her father can't save her.

When we were finally in the room, Morax grabbed my arm and walked us directly into the bathroom. I let him guide me. His unsettled feelings were becoming more evident when his claws extended and his horns appeared. The heat radiating from his skin was akin to a furnace. He walked us toward the massive walk-in shower. I stopped when he let go of me to undress.

"Morax…" I started, but he held up a hand and growled at me.

"Don't. Please don't, little lumen." His voice was desperate and shaking with rage.

Instead of responding, I untied the straps at my neck and let the silk dress fall to the floor. I wore nothing beneath it. Morax growled low in the back of his throat as his eyes drifted down my body. His forked tongue slipped out, licking his lips. I shivered and clenched my thighs beneath his hungry gaze.

The sight of him naked was like a dream, something not even my waking imagination could create. His skin was glowing red, and his chest heaved with rage. The muscles rippled across his stomach with each breath. The veins in his arms popped when he squeezed his claws into fists. Blood dripped from his palms when the claws pricked his skin.

"Stop!" I rushed toward him, and his hands instantly wrapped around my waist, smearing his blood on my skin.

His erection throbbed against my stomach. I didn't even have time to properly oggle his cock, distracted as I was by the blood dripping from his hands. My fingers traced up his thick biceps, and I stood on tiptoes to twine my hands behind his neck.

Morax dropped his forehead to mine. "I don't know if I can do this. I nearly killed them all."

"We can't yet. They're strong," I murmured, and he snarled. "You couldn't penetrate their shields, could you?"

Morax huffed. "Darren's for a few moments while he fondled my fucking mate. I didn't get much, other than hints of plans to kidnap your sister. Obscuritas members are turning up dead and they think it's her."

"I fucking hope so. I hope she kills them all," I snarled, and Morax smirked, some of the light returning to his angry eyes.

"So fierce, little lumen." His hands moved lower and cupped my ass. "Now get into the shower. I need to wash the scent of that fucker from your skin before I go insane."

Morax pulled me into the shower and set the water running to a hellish temperature. It felt divine. I wanted to wash away Darren Radnor's touch just as much as he did. For several minutes, there was a peaceful silence between us as Morax scrubbed my body with gentle touches. His claws were gone once more as he soaped my chest. My head rolled back, and I closed my eyes while he took his time massaging my breasts, kneading the soft flesh with his rough hands. He rolled my right nipple between two fingers, and I moaned.

One hand slipped lower, and my thighs clenched with desire.

"Open up for me, *mae domina*," Morax purred, and I forced my legs apart. He gently wiped the soapy washcloth between my legs. His fingers flicked my clit playfully, and I moaned again. He teased me, his movements slow and steady. Heat spread inside me, and I wanted more, but his pace never changed.

"Morax." I rasped out his name.

He leaned down and nipped at my ear. "Yes, princess?"

I whimpered as he continued to trail kisses across my collarbone. "When are you going to fuck me?"

Morax chuckled, and it was easily one of the sexiest things I've ever heard. "Is my princess eager to take my cock?"

I reached my hand down between us and wrapped it around

his length. Morax growled as I slowly stroked his shaft. His cock was fucking massive. The width alone was going to ruin me in the best way. It was thick and long, with a bulbous head. I stroked my thumb over the head, and he snarled, biting down on my neck. I gasped, taking the small pain and moaning when he licked it away.

"I want you to fuck me." I started to beg as I stroked him.

His cock throbbed in my hand, and my pussy pulsed with desire in response. My body burned for his touch, and I needed him to make me feel whole again. I never knew I could feel such aching emptiness. And I was certain only Morax could satisfy this feeling.

His cock twitched and swelled in my hand, little ridges growing down the shaft, like it was wrapped in rings. I'd seen human cocks before and this was different. The size of him was insane. And the added ridges…fuck I wanted to feel him. I licked my lips and looked up at him, our eyes colliding.

His eyes were golden and filled with desire. My heart beat erratically as he continued to look at me, his hands massaging my breasts and my own stroking his cock. The intimacy of this moment was overwhelming, and I wanted to look away. One of his hands moved to my jaw and held my face firmly so I couldn't, as if he sensed my feelings. Morax was so in tune with my every movement.

"I want more than anything to fill your sweet cunt with my cock, princess." His voice was rough and set me on fire instantly. "You are mine. This gorgeous body is mine to take. These perfect tits and that delicious pussy are mine."

I was panting now, squeezing his cock at his filthy words. My mind and body responded to his voice, begging for his touch.

"Yes. Yours. Take it. Please." I begged again, uncaring of how needy I sounded.

Morax grinned like the daemon he was. "Fuck. I love to hear your beg for my cock, princess. And it's yours. Always." He moved my hands away, grabbing my wrists and walking us backward until my back hit the shower wall. He brought my wrists up above my head and held them hostage with one hand. His claws extended, digging into the tile. His other hand drifted over my body, making me shiver.

Morax wasted no time spreading my lips and dipping a finger inside me. I moaned, my back arching as he fucked me with his finger. He added a second finger, and my moans grew louder when he curled them inside me. The palm of his hand pressed against my clit while his fingers filled my pussy.

He brought his head down, and his forked tongue flicked out, circling my left nipple. I squirmed, but his grip remained tight, holding me in place.

"You're so fucking tight, princess. It's going to feel so fucking good, this tight little cunt wrapped around my cock."

"Morax. Please," I whimpered as his hands worked me faster, pumping into me while his palm rubbed against my clit. The orgasm was building fast. My body was on fire for my daemon.

Morax brought his mouth down on my other nipple, licking and teasing. He pulled away just enough to whisper a command. "Come for me, princess."

His teeth clamped down on my nipple sharply as his fingers pumped again and again until I was screaming his name. The pain of his sharp teeth marking my skin was drowned out by the euphoria flooding my veins. His fingers moved slower, lazily milking my orgasm as my body shuddered.

"When I fuck you, little lumen, it will last for days," Morax growled, slipping his fingers from my pussy and pressing them to my lips.

I opened my mouth, and he slipped two fingers inside. I tasted my cum as he stroked my tongue, forcing me to suck while he spoke.

"The first time I fuck you, there won't be Obscuritas scum within a hundred miles of your naked flesh. They don't get to hear your screams. To bear witness to the claim I will make of your body, mind, and soul."

My mouth dried up, and I swallowed audibly at the declaration. The disappointment I felt at his slight rejection was quickly drowned out by the feral look in his eyes. As much as I wanted him to take me now, I wanted his promises for what was to come even more. He pulled his fingers from my mouth and held my face, staring into my eyes with so much feeling I thought my heart would burst.

"I'm going to hold you to that, mate." My voice was quiet, but he clearly heard that final word.

Mate. It felt impossible. Something in a fairy tale. But it was true. He was mine, and I was his.

CHAPTER FIFTEEN
Morax

As soon as the word left her perfect mouth, I nearly flipped her around and fucked her against the shower wall. *Mate.* She was claiming me. Power hummed in my veins, eager to join with hers. Instead, I brought my mouth down to hers and kissed her fiercely. I pressed into her, pinning her petite frame against the wall as I kissed the fucking life out of her. My perfect fucking mate. The desire to rip her away from this place was overwhelming. I needed to protect her. Claim her. Own her. I snarled, kissing her harder, biting her lip and drawing blood. She moaned into me as I sucked her bruised lip. Her blood was like the sweetest liquor. My veins pulsed with power as I swallowed down the smallest taste of her lumen power.

Michaela Valdis was stronger than she knew. I could taste it, the smoldering power in her blood just waiting to be unleashed. I finally pulled away, and we both heaved, sucking in oxygen.

"I need to go, little lumen. I spelled the room so no one would hear us and tweaked the camera in the hallway. They will notice eventually." No part of me wanted to leave her, but protecting her was my priority. So, I would play my role.

She nodded. "I understand. We can do this. Together. We

will play our roles for now."

I stroked her delicate face. "So brave, *mae domina*."

I quickly shut off the water and grabbed a towel to wrap her up in before getting another for myself. My cock was still hard as fuck for her, and I willed it to go down. I had a job to do now.

"Do you think you can help Tibby?" Michaela asked, running a brush through her wet hair.

I frowned. "Yes, but it will be difficult. Laszlo has fucked with her mind for quite some time."

"I want him dead. I want her to spit fucking food into his stupid mouth."

I chuckled at my fiery mate. "What a filthy mouth you have, princess. I can't wait to fuck it."

The blush in her cheeks made my cock throb, and I stalked toward her, stealing another filthy kiss. Her body instantly melted into mine, and I purred at the submission she offered me.

I pulled away, hating it, but knowing I had to go to protect us both. I gathered the guard uniform that was thrown about and redressed. Michaela pulled a set of silky pajamas from the closet and slipped them on. Seeing her in anything belonging to The Obscuritas filth made my blood boil. Soon enough, I would have her to myself and my mate would never wear clothes again. I wanted her body on display for me and only me.

Ready for duty once more, I kissed her softly and left the suite. I whispered a few words and turned the cameras back on. Technology was easy enough to manipulate. The guards also all had malleable minds. If they started to question anything, I'd simply alter their thoughts. I had to be a little more careful, though, since the Kings would also likely read the minds of their guards.

"Brother, I hope you're right about all this shit," I mumbled, wishing Phen could hear me.

We had approximately five months of this shit situation, according to my brother. When the Snow Moon rose over the winter sky, he would come. And the only way he would be able to come here would be through Seraphina. Which meant I had to keep my mate safe and her assassin sister alive and out of the Kings' hands until then. Fucking hell.

CHAPTER SIXTEEN

FIVE MONTHS LATER

Michaela

I walked the hall with Morax remaining quiet at my side. We were both agitated. A radio call came through requesting my presence in The Study immediately. Morax couldn't get anything specific from the other guards, so we walked in silence, preparing for anything that might come.

It had been five miserable months since I was taken prisoner. Well, not completely miserable. Having Morax by my side was the only thing keeping me sane. He was making progress with Tibby, especially after a surprising revelation. Tibby was able to withstand so much torture because she had protection. Morax was still working it out, but he thought Seraphina had given her some kind of shield. He couldn't reach that far into her memories to figure out how my sister did it, not without scrambling Tibby's brain. I wasn't sure if it was a blessing or a curse, coming out of the fog Laszlo held her in. She still had to come here and cower like a slave.

As much as I hated Tibby leaving to go spy on my sister, I was grateful she could still leave the mansion and get away from Laszlo. And I was honestly a little pissed Seraphina didn't realize her friend was basically an Obscuritas robot. The Kings used what power they had to remove any injuries, but still. Didn't she notice something was wrong with her friend?

Gremory was also still missing. Morax was having trouble sensing the daemon and said Grem must have a very powerful witch aiding him to cloak him so fully. I wasn't sure what that meant. He still hadn't turned us in, or outed Morax to the stupid cult leaders. Morax did listen in on his captain's thoughts, and a new guard was joining them soon. He had a feeling it was Grem.

Thankfully, my sister was wreaking havoc among The Obscuritas, killing more of their men and infuriating the Kings. And even more, their sons were apparently with her too. This was shocking news for Morax and myself. How could she shack up with Obscuritas Princes? It felt like a betrayal. But then again, the Princes were defying their fathers, so were they on our side now? Everything was so fucking confusing. Hushed and excited voices floated into the hallway as we approached The Study. I entered the room first, keeping my face blank as I noted the three Kings in the room looking entirely too happy. Darren came toward me immediately, and I couldn't help flinching away from him.

The action lit a fire in his eyes. He preferred it when I resisted. He grabbed me around the waist and pulled me close, wrapping one hand around my throat and gripping my ass with the other so hard it brought tears to my eyes. "We've got her now, baby. Your sister is as good as ours."

I nearly choked on my next breath, and my mouth went dry. I wasn't ready for this. I resisted the urge to turn to Morax. I knew he'd be raging right now with Darren's hands all over me.

Things with Darren were actually easier now. Morax was able to gain access to his mind enough to alter his thoughts. It happened around Christmas. Snow was falling, and I watched in awe at the beauty of it from my bedroom window. Darren Radnor came into the room, and I could tell things were different. He came at me fast, tossing me on the bed and pinning me beneath him. He was going to fuck me as a present. The other Kings apparently agreed. They wanted him to get me pregnant.

I lost it. I screamed and kicked at him, refusing. My struggle only turned him on further. When Morax burst into the room, Darren's mind was so focused on raping me that his shields were down. Morax pounced and took control within seconds. From that night on, Darren came to my room, every single night. And while he had visions of us fucking, he was actually laid out on the floor, slack-jawed and lost to Morax's power.

It was cleverly done, but I still hated having to pretend Darren was actually fucking me. At the dinners, he would grope me and brag to the others about owning my virgin pussy. He thought he knew what I tasted like. He was a sick fuck. I hated the things he thought he did to me. Morax hated it even more, not wanting anyone near my body, even if it was only in their mind.

The only snag in our plan was that I obviously wasn't getting pregnant. Darren was growing increasingly angry, and I knew we'd have to figure something out soon. Morax refused to even consider knocking me up himself when I suggested it. I didn't love the idea either, but we were running out of options. He flat out refused, reciting his earlier declaration of how and when he would claim me. And telling me no child of ours would be born like this.

I never really thought about children. It seemed like a silly daydream. But the thought of having a baby with Morax made my blood sing and the butterflies in my stomach go insane.

"Did you hear me, baby?" Darren whispered close to my ear, and I tried not to gag. "We're bringing her here soon. You'll be together again."

Samuel laughed. "Finally. I've been growing bored."

Laszlo smirked. "Yes. Our new ally is proving very useful."

New ally? The Kings must have someone else on their side. Who could it be? I didn't ask, remaining silent. It was easier not to blow my cover as a broken, submissive girl if I didn't speak.

Several guards entered the room with Tibby in tow. She looked like a cat backed into a corner, trying desperately to find a way out. One of the stronger barriers Laszlo put in her mind made it impossible to tell Seraphina anything. So even when she was more lucid, more herself, she still couldn't warn my sister. Tibby immediately went to Laszlo and dropped to her knees before him, saying nothing.

Laszlo looked past my shoulder at Morax, and my stomach dropped. "Guard, come forward. My slave nearly fucked everything to shit. She needs to be taught a lesson and remember who she belongs to."

My body went rigid. I had no idea what Laszlo had planned, but I knew it was going to be something I wouldn't be able to watch. Darren Radnor was now wrapped around me, his hard-on pressing into my ass as his hands pinched and teased my skin. My flesh was hot, and my body was humming with energy. Whatever was about to happen, I did not want it to. I had to stop this.

Morax calmly walked to Laszlo and stood before the stupid Obscuritas King.

Laszlo pat Tibby's head like an asshole. "You are loyal to me, aren't you?"

Tibby nodded, her voice quivering with uncertainty. "Yes, master."

"Of course you are." Laszlo turned to Morax. "I want you to suck this guard's cock. Prove to me and everyone here what a perfect slave you are for your master."

Absolutely fucking not. My blood was burning me from the inside out as Tibby crawled closer to Morax and knelt before him. My mate stood there, unmoving, as Tibby went to undo his belt. *I'm going to die.* I couldn't watch this. It would tear my heart out. Jealous rage flooded my mind. I hated that I was jealous. I knew this wasn't her fault. And how could Morax say no? But I just couldn't watch this. Angry tears burned my eyes as Darren continued to touch me everywhere, but I was numb to him in this moment. My tunnel vision saw only Tibby's shaking hands undoing the belt of my mate to suck his cock in front of me.

Morax's hand suddenly snapped out and grabbed her wrist. I sucked in a breath as the room went silent.

"The bitch doesn't deserve to suck cock." His voice was foreign in this human form as he spoke slowly, his eyes on Tibby. He pulled out the gun strapped to his hip. "Suck my gun, slave."

Laszlo watched as Tibby opened her mouth and slowly

began sucking the barrel of the gun. Tears filled her eyes as her head bobbed over the length of the gun. Shame washed over me for my jealous thoughts. Morax was saving us all from Laszlo's demand, and yet Tibby still paid the price. I hated this. I hated the Kings, and I wished they would all fucking die.

The three Obscuritas Kings chuckled at her misery.

Laszlo cleared his throat and ordered her to stop. "Enough for now, slave. Go to your cage and wait for the final instructions."

Tibby stood and quickly left the room. Laszlo narrowed his eyes on my mate. Morax dropped his head, playing the obedient guard.

"While your idea was creative, I gave my slave a direct order and you forced her to disobey. Perhaps you would enjoy watching me punish her then?"

Morax nodded. "If you wish, sir."

Laszlo stepped in closer. "Do not do something like that again."

"Yes, sir."

Darren chuckled in my ear, his breath fanning against my neck and making my skin crawl. "I want to watch her get punished. Don't you, baby?"

I refused to respond. No matter what I'd say, he'd enjoy it too much. Darren grabbed my neck and turned me around to face him. His eyes had an evil glint to them I definitely did not like.

"It's time to move you into my room. Samuel has given me some new toys. As soon as your sister arrives, we'll try them out." His grip on my neck tightened, preventing me from breathing.

"I cannot wait to hear you scream. I've been dying to see your pretty face all screwed up in pain. It's going to make fucking you so much more pleasurable for me. I think that's why I haven't knocked you up yet. I need your screams."

I was starting to see spots, his grip on my neck too tight. I clawed at his hands, desperate for air. The room darkened further, and I was sure I would pass out when he finally let go. I dropped to the floor, coughing and sucking down precious oxygen. The heat of Morax's anger burned behind me, and I knew he was close to breaking. That was not an option. So I stood up again and squared my shoulders, facing Darren.

"Darren, take your unruly prize to your room," Laszlo cut in. "Do not kill her, for fuck's sake. I need Seraphina's submission before you ruin the girl."

Darren laughed, and Samuel joined. Samuel left the room, and Darren grabbed my arm, pulling me toward the door. Morax moved to follow, but Laszlo stopped him.

"No. I need you to run an errand for me. We are securing our new ally. Your captain will give you the details. Return to your post outside Darren's room once you are finished."

Morax nodded. His eyes flashed in my direction, filled with rage and terrified concern. I sent him strength, willing him to come back to me as soon as he could. I had no doubt Darren planned to hurt me, and I could handle that. But if Morax didn't come back in time, he'd finally get to take my virginity too.

The walk to his bedroom felt like walking to my own funeral.

This was death row, and at the end of this hall was my electric chair. My lethal injection. My end. Who I was before this moment would be erased. Destroyed. Darren Radnor whispered horrible things in my ear. His grip on my bicep bruised, and I sent my mind away to ignore the pain. I didn't want to be here when he began whatever he had planned for me.

Laszlo told him not to ruin me completely, because if he did, my sister would never surrender to them. But that didn't make me feel any better. The Kings had decades of practice torturing, raping, and ruining anyone they wanted. Darren would have little trouble ravaging my mind and body and hiding the scars from prying eyes.

A guard stood in front of the double doors at the end of the hall. He opened the door, barely sparing me a glance. Not that he would help, he belonged to the Kings. Darren shoved me into the room. Everything in his suite was decorated with deep reds and blacks. The walls were lined with portraits of people in various stages of torture, their faces wrought with pain. I had no doubt they were real people. I noted the rolling cart full of his "toys." Some of them were familiar, sex toys like dildos, plugs, and whips. But there were others with spikes and chains, and some kind of machine that looked like it would electrocute his victims. Bile rose in my throat, and I swallowed it down, taking deep breaths and willing my mind to save itself from what was coming. I turned around, standing in front of his bed.

Darren Radnor slapped me hard across the face, knocking me to the floor. The shock at least held the pain at bay for a few seconds. I tasted blood in my mouth. Fuck this guy and fuck the Kings. I looked up at him, rage and hate filling my eyes, and spat in his face.

He smiled. "That's good, baby. I love the fighters. It feels so much better when they break."

For as bulky as he was, Darren moved quickly. He grabbed me by the hair and yanked my head back harshly. In the next moment, electricity shot through my body like lightning. I fell to the floor, my body going limp from the high-voltage taser. I couldn't stop the groans of pain from leaving my lips.

Darren moved away to roll something toward me. It was made of wood and vaguely familiar. A medieval imprisonment device called a pillory. He unlatched the top piece of wood and lifted me up roughly, placing my wrists in the smaller grooves and my head in the center. Then he brought the top piece back down and locked me into the device. Pain coursed through my body like tiny knives, and I gritted my teeth, unable to do anything but take it.

Morax, please hurry.

"Now, let's remove these clothes. I want to see all of you. How every muscle in your little body twitches in agony under my ministrations." Darren's evil smile was horrible, and I stared into the distance, shutting down and trying to ignore his words. "I promised Samuel he could come in and see how I used his toys. But I wanted you all to myself for the first few hours."

Darren walked behind me as he spoke, a sharp knife in his hand. I was positioned on my knees, at eye level with his waistline and unable to move my head to see where he was. He began cutting and tearing away my dress, my bra, and my underwear. He poked the blade into my skin, not enough to make me bleed, but enough to let me know he was in charge now.

"Such pretty, milky white skin. We're going to cover it in blood. Every inch of your body will bear a mark from me. I will open your flesh one piece at a time. What should we fill your pussy with first? I can't decide if I want to watch you bounce on my cock or one of these rather painful looking dildos. Samuel is a sick fuck, isn't he?"

I barely registered what he was saying. My mind was going away. I was back at the warehouse, dancing with Morax. I closed my eyes and swayed to the beat of the music, falling into the heat of his body against mine.

Darren was shouting now. He tased me again, and distantly, my body convulsed and strained against the prison I was locked into. He gripped my hair, and pain shot through my shoulders as he pulled my head up and stretched my neck further. The next moment, I felt something soft in my mouth. His cock was in my mouth.

"If you bite down, I will stick this fucking knife in your ass and tear you apart. Now suck your King's cock," Darren growled.

I didn't bite down, but I didn't suck either. I did nothing. My mind was gone, safe at the warehouse with my daemon while this vile monster fucked my mouth with his stubby little cock. Tears pricked my eyes as he choked me. He leaned down and pinched my nipples so hard I cried out. He moaned, his little cock throbbing at the sound of my pain.

The beat of the music in my head grew louder, and I went away again, drifting into darkness with only the music to keep my mind from shattering.

A voice roared in the distance. I recognized it. My daemon.

My mind must have been bringing him to life. I wanted to call out to him. Voices were shouting. I took a deep breath, realizing there was no longer a cock in my mouth. Something was wrong. I needed to get back to my body. But I was so far away now. It was safe here. The music called to me in the dark, and I followed it away. Far, far away.

CHAPTER SEVENTEEN

Morax

There was a guard standing at Darren's door, and I quickly overpowered his human mind. I ordered him to come into the room and draw his weapon. He would die, but I couldn't have him wandering the mansion and giving me up. When I stepped into the room, the scene before me was something conjured in my very worst nightmares. My mate was naked and locked into a pillory. Her eyes were glazed, and Darren Radnor's cock was in her mouth.

I completely lost my shit. My daemon form exploded out of me, wings, horns, and all. My skin glowed red as my power grew, and I knew my eyes had turned solid gold with the force of it. I had enough presence of mind to put a sound barrier around the room before I roared my fury and ripped the piece of shit from my mate. I couldn't think, didn't stop to consider the consequences. I slashed his puny cock from his body, and blood sprayed across the room. He screamed, but I didn't give him much time for that either. My claws dug into his chest, and his mouth opened in another soundless scream of pain as I ripped his heart from his body. Fire spilled from my fingertips, and his body turned to dust in seconds. The entire gruesome affair ended in less than two minutes.

The guard stood in the corner, his eyes wide with shock. I sent a thought to his mind, and in the next second, he pressed his gun to his temple and pulled the trigger.

I turned back to Michaela. She wasn't moving, and her eyes were still glazed over. She clearly sent her mind away to save herself. I ripped the lock from the pillory and opened it, gently pulling her into my arms. She was naked and had several burns from what was likely a taser. Rage burned through me, and I wanted to murder that fucker all over again. She was covered in his blood. The human piece of shit made a mess before he died.

My daemon form slowly retreated, not fully, but enough for me to move to the bathroom. I held Michaela close as I started the water to fill the tub. I stepped into it, cradling her against my chest as the warm water rose around us. I kissed her gently and whispered her name. She wasn't moving or reacting to me, and my heart beat erratically.

"She's gone, Morax." A voice from the doorway startled me, and I snarled, horns and claws snapping out. *Gremory.*

"I will fucking rip you apart if you come any closer," I snarled at him, my fangs on display.

He was at least smart enough not to challenge me and remained in his human form. Gremory's hands rose in surrender. "I'm here to help, jackass. You need to go into her mind. She sent herself away."

"I know what I need to do," I growled at him. "I fucking know what my mate needs."

He shrugged, crossing his arms and leaning against the doorway.

I turned back to my mate, pressing my lips to her forehead,

and whispered, "I'm coming, little lumen. Let me in."

My eyes closed, and I opened my own mind to find hers.

Her mind was full of darkness. But there was music. It reminded me of the warehouse I found her in so many nights ago. She was there again, dancing. Her eyes were closed as she lost herself to the music. I came up behind her and wrapped my arms around her waist. She didn't speak, just pressed her warm body against mine and whimpered.

"I'm here, princess. I will always be here." I licked her neck and held her tightly, swaying to the music in her mind.

"Morax," she whispered, and the pain in her voice cut my heart to pieces. "Where are you?"

I turned her body around to face me and held her tight. Her eyes were full of pain when she looked up at me.

"I'm here, little lumen. Come back to me. Michaela. My mate."

Her chest heaved against my own as I brought us out of her mind. Her eyes flitted, and she whimpered again. The sound was music to my ears in that moment. She was coming back to me. Her body jerked, and I held her tight.

"It's me, little lumen. Just you and me," I murmured softly, willing her to relax.

She turned, and her beautiful eyes captured mine. "You took too long."

Her broken voice turned my insides to ash. "I am so fucking sorry. I will never leave you again. Never."

She nodded and curled into me. "Good. Can you find me some soap? I need to wash my mouth out for a year."

I know she wanted me to laugh, but I couldn't. My skin glowed red and my eyes burned with rage at the vision of that filth fucking her mouth.

"I wouldn't make jokes just yet, Michaela. Your mate is in a heightened state of violence,"

Gremory drawled from his position against the door.

Michaela's head snapped in his direction, and I squeezed her tightly. He could not see any of her body while I had her cocooned against my chest.

"Why are you here?" she demanded, and the strength in her voice settled my rage a miniscule amount.

"I'm here to help." Gremory pulled several towels from a closet and set them at the edge of the tub. "Despite our previous encounter, we are not enemies. Why don't you get out of the bloody water and we can chat?"

I gathered Michaela in my arms and stepped out of the tub. Grem held out a towel, his face turned away. I took it from him and wrapped it around her body as best I could. I refused to let go of her. The mate bond raged, and even having Gremory so close to her was difficult for me.

I stalked out of the bathroom and Gremory followed. The bloody mess of Darren Radnor was gone, as was the guard.

Gremory noted my cocked eyebrow and smiled. "A piece offering. I cleaned up the mess. Can't have the other Kings finding one of their own ripped to shreds in his bedroom."

"I'm going to rip them all apart," I growled. " I don't give a fuck about the plans. I'll burn this whole fucking mansion to the ground right now."

Grem rolled his eyes. "Let's not. You do remember your

non-evil brother, sweet Phenex, don't you? He needs this ritual to happen. You know that."

I snarled. Of course I fucking knew that. But right now, I was so fucking angry it didn't matter.

"Her sister would die too, you know."

Gremory's words slithered through the rage clouding my head, and I took several deep breaths. Michaela would be heartbroken if the only sister she had left was killed. Satiating my bloodlust wasn't worth hurting my mate or the people she loved most. I'd sooner cut my own heart out than cause her anymore harm. My failure to save her from that piece of shit would haunt me for eternity.

I sat in an armchair, refusing to have my mate anywhere near that fucker's bed. I held her close with the towels wrapped around her petite frame. She snuggled into me and closed her eyes. Her heart beat at a regular pace, and I purred deep in my chest, an ounce of relief sinking in that she felt safe in my arms.

"Tell me your plan, Grem. And if it isn't fucking foolproof, I will rip your heart out with the rest of them." I stared at him, daring him to doubt my threat.

The daemon in him rumbled, preparing for a fight, and his human form flickered. He settled quickly, rolling his eyes and crossing his arms. He wore a guard uniform similar to my own. It irritated me that he was working for them, and all these months, I was unable to track him down. Part of me hoped he had died from the knife I stabbed into his chest when we fought at that warehouse. Obviously, I did not get my wish. Perhaps it was divine intervention that my blade missed his heart.

"I won't start from the beginning. You obviously know Belial is making moves to take over your father's throne. We thought your father was a treat, but Belial is worse. He's rounding up any of the Malefica he can find and—"

I cut him off. "Why is he rounding up the witches? And why do you care?"

Gremory's mouth flattened, and a muscle ticked in his jaw. He was hiding information from me.

I snarled at him. "If we're going to work together, I need to know. Everything."

Gremory took several steps toward me. His skin began to glow a dark green, and his horns appeared. "What I share with you is my choice. And I will kill you if I find out you used it against me."

I eyed him warily. He looked ready to murder me. And he was losing control of his daemon form. A scent wafted toward me I hadn't caught before. Sulfur and seawater.

"Grem. Don't tell me you're fucking a witch."

He snarled, his fangs dropping and his eyes glowing bright silver. I noticed a slim silver and hematite bracelet around his wrist and narrowed my eyes in understanding. He was stronger because this witch was aiding him.

I chuckled. "You mated with a witch."

"Are we really going to talk shit on mate bonds when you hold a human hybrid in your arms?" Grem smirked, gaining control, and I growled at him.

This working relationship was going to get us both killed. "Fine. No more mate insults. What is my brother doing with the Malefica?"

The Malefica were akin to witches of the human world, but

their power was far greater. Daemons and lumens rarely crossed paths with them after we collectively wiped them out. It was centuries ago, and only recently have they regained numbers. Their royals were called The Mal-Regia. I suspected Grem's mate was one of the royals.

He shook his head. "I don't know. My mate is here. She's been here since Aurora cut off access between our world and the humans'. She left for reasons I will not share just yet. I fled Caligo under the guise of helping Belial recruit more of the hybrids to his cause. That's what he's using this lame ass cult for."

I sighed. Belial was no idiot, and Grem was still hiding things. For now, we had no choice but to trust him. And I prayed whatever plan Phenex had would pan out. "Phen says he has the ritual under control. Whatever goes down come the full moon, it will be in our favor."

Grem ran his fingers through his long, blond hair and sighed. "I fucking hope so. No offense, but Phen is one crazy fucker with the attention span of a goldfish."

I raised one eyebrow. "And how short is the attention span of a goldfish?"

Grem smiled. "About seven seconds."

I smirked. "Too long."

He huffed a laugh. I loved my younger brother dearly. But there was not a single instance in our lives where he followed through with a plan, and then said plan actually worked. The only reason I trusted this particular plan was because of the girl in my arms. Phen couldn't tell me how he knew, or who he met with, but the daughters of Aurora Valdis were the key to defeating my father and my brother.

"What do we do now? The other Kings will notice one of their number is missing." I couldn't bring myself to regret what I did, but we were now in a very dangerous situation.

Grem nodded. "And then there were two… I have a plan. You are going to be the new Darren Radnor." He pulled out a small vial, and I could smell the rancid blood of that fucker from here.

I shook my head. "This is a horrible plan."

Grem shrugged. "It's the best one we've got. The Kings need to think Radnor is still alive, and you need to keep your mate close."

I looked down at my sleeping mate. Her brows were furrowed, and she clung to me while she dreamt. I never wanted her to see that fucker again, but this was a solid plan. "Fine. I need to warn her first. Have some of her things brought to this room while I speak with her."

Gremory left quickly, and I brushed my fingers against my beautiful mate's cheek. She was going to hate this. But she was also stronger than even she realized. And I would make sure she knew it.

CHAPTER EIGHTEEN
Michaela

My dreams were more like nightmares as Darren Radnor's voice grated inside my head. I didn't want to dream about him. Didn't want to think about him ever again. But unfortunately, trauma didn't work like that. The scent of my daemon and his deep voice was pulling me out of my nightmare. I clung to the sound of his soothing words and leaned into his touch.

"Hello, little lumen," he murmured, stroking my cheek.

Images flashed in my mind of his full daemon form exploding into the room. There was blood everywhere. I looked around and realized we were alone and there was not a spec of gore to be found.

"Where is Gremory? What happened?" My voice was hoarse. I think I was screaming, in the end.

Morax brought his arm down and began massaging my shoulder in slow and steady movements. Everything about him right now was calming.

"He's getting some clothes and things for you. We…have a plan. One that will keep us together and the Kings in the dark about their dead friend," Morax growled, his rage clearly not fully under control. He also sounded hesitant.

I sat up a little in his lap and looked at him. I wasn't going to like this plan, that was obvious. But I fully believed he wouldn't even consider it if it wasn't absolutely necessary. "Tell me the plan."

Morax explained it to me, and I was right, I hated this plan. He would become the monster in my nightmares. We would have to stay in the monster's room. My body started to shake, and bile rose in my throat. I closed my eyes and leaned back into my daemon, taking deep breaths. He smelled of the mountains, a mix of snow, spruce, and pine with a smoky aftertaste. My body settled, and I was tempted to lick his chest.

He chuckled, and a low purr built in his chest, soothing me. "I am glad to see your body remembers me, mate."

My skin flushed, and I was also filled with relief that I could still feel desire for him. I was terrified Darren had stolen that from me. *No, I wouldn't let him.* He would be forgotten. Hopefully sooner rather than later.

"I like the way you smell," I whispered, nuzzling him and breathing deep again.

Morax growled, and his hand circled my throat delicately. He brought his nose down to my ear and flicked his forked tongue against the soft flesh. "You smell almost as delicious as you taste, princess. Like sunlight and the ocean. Not your oceans, but the deep, unexplored waters of my homeland. Full of life and immense power. You're the strongest creature I've ever met."

I shivered in his arms and turned to stare up at his liquid gold gaze. I liked him better in his true daemon form. "Not as strong as you."

His hand tightened slightly around my throat. "Stronger, *mae domina*. And I cannot wait to witness your full power. Kings will fall at your feet."

"I like the sound of that." I was acutely aware of my naked body loosely covered in towels and so close to his raw heat. I stretched, trying to turn and face him, and immediately winced. My body was sore. And while I healed fast, my stomach where Darren zapped me with that awful fucking taser was still bruised and tender.

Morax noticed my pain instantly. "Relax, little lumen. Let your body heal. Let me hold you a little longer."

My heart melted at his sweet words. I brushed my thumb against his bottom lip, and his tongue snaked out to taste me. "You're a big softie, aren't you?"

Morax huffed, and his fangs descended. His eyes filled with heat, capturing mine and refusing to let go. "I am your creature, my beautiful mate. Whichever form you need of me, I will become."

My heart beat rapidly in my chest at the intensity of his stare and the mesmerizing words my daemon muttered. Mine. This beast with claws and fangs and power I barely understood was mine. And yet he made me feel powerful. The half-lumen, half-human girl with zero self-control. He belonged to me. I don't think I'd ever get used to it.

I broke our locked gaze and studied the room, Darren's room, and crinkled my nose. "I hate everything about this room."

The door opened, and I jumped, but Morax held me tight, unphased. Of course he would know if anyone was coming, good or bad. Gremory strolled into the room, a rolling trunk trailing behind him. He dropped it with a thud at the foot of the bed.

"A few of your things, lumen princess." Gremory offered a mock bow, and Morax growled at him. The sly daemon remained unphased. He pulled a small vial from his pocket and set it on top of the trunk. "A single drop will suffice. The illusion will last for approximately twelve hours before you need to take another. So try not to get caught out without it."

Morax nodded. "Understood."

Gremory turned toward the door, his hand on the knob, and paused. When he turned back, he whispered a few words, and I watched in awe as his hands glowed emerald green. I blinked, and suddenly the entire room was redecorated. The reds and black were replaced with deep, forest greens and warm golds. The horrible photos of torture victims were replaced with beautiful landscape paintings. The entire room was transformed into a beautiful oasis of rich, soothing colors and a calming atmosphere.

My mouth dropped open as I absorbed our new room. "This is wonderful."

Gremory smiled, but it didn't reach his eyes. "A little bit of home. I am sorry Morax and I were not here sooner."

I swallowed and nodded. Words were too much.

Morax hugged me closer and offered a small smile to the daemon. "Thank you, Grem."

He nodded curtly and left us.

Morax stood, carrying me easily, as if I weighed no more than a pillow, and helped me into our new bed. I shivered, pulling the covers over my naked body. He climbed into the bed behind me, wrapping his naked body around my own. His skin was hot and warmed me instantly.

I wiggled against him, and he growled.

"You need to rest, princess."

Maybe I did, but having a yummy naked daemon in my bed was hardly sleep-inducing.

"Don't orgasms help you sleep better? I think I read that somewhere."

My daemon chuckled, his breath dusting against my neck, and I shivered for a whole new reason. His mouth dropped to my shoulder, and his fangs nipped gently at my bare skin.

"I told you, princess. The first time I fuck you, it will last all day. There will be no one around us for miles. I want every moan I coax from your perfect body all to myself."

I couldn't help the whimper that escaped my lips at his words. I wanted him to fuck me. I wanted that reality. "You're such a tease."

Morax growled. He slipped one hand beneath the pillow my head lay on and curled his arm around my chest, holding me tightly to him. His other hand traced down my arm, my lower back, and the curve of my ass. He purred, and the rumble of it sent heat straight to my core. Morax gently gripped my thigh and pushed my leg forward, bending my knee and giving him access to my soaked pussy. Because I was soaked. He was barely touching me, and arousal coated my inner thighs.

His hand smoothed over my ass until his fingers found my core. He slipped two digits between my lips and groaned.

"Mate. You're so wet for me."

He growled the words, and I moaned as he gently slid his fingers back and forth, exploring, coating my thighs in my arousal. I squirmed, needing more, and the arm around my chest tightened.

"Be still, princess. I will give you what you need, but only if you promise to rest."

I murmured my consent, and his hands stopped.

"Yes. Yes. I promise. Please don't stop."

Morax laughed quietly and began moving his fingers again, circling my clit. "I love to hear you beg, princess. Tell me what you need."

I moaned again as he slipped a single finger inside me. "I need you. All of you. But for now I'll settle for your hands. And your mouth."

Morax growled, and his cock twitched against my backside. "*Mae domina*, your mind is as depraved as my own."

I wiggled my ass against his cock and clenched around his fingers. "Let the daemon out, Morax. I want to play with him."

Morax pulled his fingers out of me, and I started to cry out. Before I could, he pressed the soaked digits against my lips. "Taste."

My pussy throbbed, and I obeyed, opening my mouth for him. He pressed two fingers against my tongue, and I tasted the sweet and salty arousal coating his hand. I licked and sucked, imagining I was sucking his cock instead. I needed him to know how much I still wanted that. Wanted him. Morax's deep purr turned into a growl as he pulled his hand away.

"Greedy little lumen." He whispered the words and nipped my neck. Morax gently released my body from his hold and rolled me onto my back. He moved between my legs, and I dropped my thighs to the side, opening for him. My body responded to him so willingly. I wanted him to see me. The rush of power I felt when he looked at me with those daemon eyes made my head spin.

His nostrils flared, and his eyes glowed in the dark room. "Fuck, princess. I'm completely addicted to the sight of your cunt, so fucking wet and needy for me."

I swallowed, unable to speak, and licked my lips. His gaze flicked to my mouth and back between my legs. He dropped his head down and gently kissed the soft mound of flesh below my belly button. His kisses moved lower, and I started to squirm.

Morax lifted his head, and his golden eyes pierced through my soul. "Don't move, princess. Or else I will stop."

I nodded, my mouth dry and words unable to escape my lips. The nightmares were fading fast, and my daemon's mouth was erasing them with every stroke of his wicked tongue. He flicked the forked tip against my clit, and I moaned. I fisted my hands in the sheets, remembering I was supposed to be still and suddenly finding that task to be impossible.

Morax lapped at my soaked core with lazy strokes, murmuring praises between every flick of his tongue. My body was on fire, and I was ready to beg.

"Morax, please," I whimpered, using all of my strength to hold still beneath his wicked mouth.

"Yes, princess? Please what? Tell your mate what you need of him." His words were deep and laced with desire.

My pussy clenched, and I cried out as he circled my clit. "I need to come. Please make me come."

"As you wish, *mae domina*," he murmured.

I could no longer speak as his mouth fully came down on me. His claws grazed up my thighs, and I sucked in a breath when he slid a finger inside me while his tongue teased my clit. I braced myself for the feel of his sharp claws, but my daemon retracted them before pumping his finger inside me, curling up to hit the firework-inducing spot within me. I cried out as he added a second finger, pumping slow and steady.

My thighs trembled, and I was begging again.

Morax chuckled against my pussy, and his hot breath fanned against my clit. "The sound of your moans is like a siren song, princess. I could listen to you come undone for me endlessly."

I mewled as his pace increased. The sounds coming out of me should have been embarrassing, but hearing his praise and the low purr building in his chest set fire to my insides and I could think of nothing to be ashamed of.

"Come for me, princess. Clench your pretty cunt around my fingers and let me feel you." Morax growled his demands, and I acquiesced.

His fingers curled against that spot over and over, and as his mouth clamped down on my clit, I screamed my release, the orgasm rushing like a tidal wave through my body. My pussy clutched his fingers tightly, and he pumped them slowly, drawing out my pleasure.

"That's it, little lumen. You take my fingers so well. You're going to take my cock just as good."

I had no words left in me, and my body was floating on a cloud. Morax lapped at my pussy for another minute, growling his pleasure at the mess I made and refusing to move until he

licked every last drop of my cum.

I shivered with pleasure, my hand reaching down to lace my fingers in his dark wavy hair. "I want your cock. I want to feel you inside me."

My daemon growled with pleasure, and his eyes snapped to mine, filled with desire. "You will, princess."

My eyes started to close, overcome with exhaustion, and Morax slipped from the bed. He returned from the bathroom with a warm cloth and gently wiped my body down. Then he wrapped me up in the covers and curled his body against mine.

Tomorrow would be a test of our skills in deception. He would become a monstrous King, and I would be his broken toy. But I was not broken. And the daemon at my back was no cruel king. He was my mate. And their ruination.

CHAPTER NINETEEN
Michaela

When Morax stepped out of the bathroom, I almost vomited. I was strong and I was unbroken, but seeing Darren Radnor stand before me almost took me out. I gasped, and my legs wobbled. When he ran to me, I almost screamed.

He gripped my arms gently. "It's me, *mae domina*. He is gone. I wear his face, but Darren Radnor is gone. He cannot hurt you."

I nodded, swallowing audibly. "I know."

Morax stared back at me, letting his daemon eyes show through. The golden color brought some life back to my nearly stopped heart.

"I have to go play my part. I will choose Gremory as the guard to watch this room. We will go down to breakfast, so they can see you, but then I will return you to this room, and I need you to stay here. No one will enter."

I nodded. "Better chain me up or something. That fucker would."

Morax snarled, and I had to agree. The idea of being Darren's pet made my stomach curdle. He sifted through Darren's closet and found a leather collar with spikes on the outside. There was a metal loop to attach the leash.

I wore a strapless red dress, the soft fabric brushing against the floor. The slit was higher than I liked, nearly giving everyone a view of my lacy black thong when I walked. But it looked like something Darren would want me to wear. And the red, I suppose, looked pretty with my long, blonde hair waving down my back.

Morax gently lifted my hair over my right shoulder so he could clasp the collar around my neck. His fingers brushed against my collarbone, and I shivered. Maybe I didn't love wearing a collar for Darren, but being tied up and at the mercy of my daemon was another story entirely.

He chuckled, and my face flushed. "I may not be able to read your thoughts entirely, mate. But I can smell your arousal from here. If you want me to tie you up, you need only ask."

I turned around and faced him, our hungry gazes clashing. "Add it to the list, when the kings are dead."

Morax attached the leash to the collar then placed the end of the lead into my hand. He bent my fingers around it and brought my closed fist to his mouth, kissing the top of my hand reverently.

"I am your creature to command, and the leash you have wrapped around my soul is more powerful than this trinket will ever be." He looked down at me, his eyes glowing. "I cannot kiss your sweet mouth wearing this face. It would hurt us both."

My eyes watered at his declaration and the devastation I saw on his face. I wanted to kiss him and comfort him, but he was right. I didn't want to kiss this face, even if I could see my daemon shining through its eyes.

"Let's get this fucking day over with then." I squared my shoulders and handed him the leash.

There weren't any guards outside the bedroom, and we walked in silence to the dining room. I took several deep breaths and forced my face to look haunted.

It wasn't too difficult. I let the memories of Darren's torture flood my mind, and the disgust I felt when he touched me clouded my features.

The other Kings were seated at the table already. I noted Tibby's absence at Laszlo's feet and wondered where he was keeping her.

Samuel eyed me curiously and frowned. "Why didn't you let me join you yesterday? I heard her screams and was getting jealous."

Morax snarled. I had a feeling this was going to be harder for him than it was me. "Her screams belong to me. I've taken a liking to her pain, and I won't be sharing. Go find your own toy."

Laszlo smirked. "Samuel, you can't be surprised. He's wanted the girl for years now."

Samuel rolled his eyes but looked otherwise unbothered. He rarely showed his emotions. His face was a mask of in-difference, and when I looked in his eyes, the blank gaze of a true psychopath stared back at me. I quickly dropped my gaze, needing him to think I was terrified. But inside, I was raging. The death of these assholes could not come soon enough.

"Now that you've graced us with your presence, Darren, we can get on with our planning," Laszlo cut in, getting straight to business.

I slumped in my seat as servants brought out our food. I

wasn't in the mood to eat, so I pushed the eggs and sausages around on the plate and continued to look glum. Morax tugged on my leash, and I gasped, looking up at him.

"Eat," he commanded. "Can't have you dying so soon because you starve yourself."

The angry retort was so close to slipping past my lips, but I held it back. He was getting smacked for that later. I did as he asked, though, and shoved some scrambled eggs in my mouth.

Laszlo continued. "Tabitha has returned to her place at Seraphina's side, and with our sons. She will set things in motion. Devon will handle things from there."

Devon was one of The Obscuritas Princes, but I thought the Princes were rebelling against their fathers. *Now he was turning against my sister?*

"And are we certain of Devon's compliance?" Morax asked, framing the question in a way that wouldn't draw attention to our ignorance.

Laszlo nodded. "Samuel was able to convince him of Seraphina's betrayal. The fabricated memories are enough for now. If he does cave to that whore again, we will use our other asset to bring him to heel."

Morax nodded. We needed to know what this other asset was, but there was no way to ask without looking suspicious. "Very well. What do you need from me today? I am eager to play with my new toy."

Laszlo rolled his eyes, standing from his seat at the table. "If all goes well, Seraphina will be ours by tomorrow night. Keep the girl looking as she does now until then. Seraphina needs to see her relatively unblemished. My sons are having a party this evening. Go with Samuel to assure Devon is behaving the way we need. We have spies attending, but I need to be certain this all goes according to plan."

Morax nodded and also stood, yanking on the leash enough to force me to stand. "I'll be ready shortly."

Before we could leave the room, several guards entered through a door on the far side of the room, and one of them was Gremory. I'd seen his human form and recognized him immediately. His pace was hurried, but not as tortured as the guard walking directly toward the Kings. This one's face was disturbed, and sweat dripped down his hairline. And I recognized him. Tony. The prick was on my list.

Clearly something bad had happened. The guards stopped before reaching the table and bowed to each of the Kings.

"What's happened?" Samuel asked first.

The front guard hesitated. "Professor Lehmann is dead, sir. There is little evidence. The cameras in and around his home have been tampered with. The girl he had is also gone."

Samuel cursed, and Laszlo frowned. "Is that all?"

He shook his head. "No. We were able to find messages between a burner phone and a woman, Ms. Audrey Kingston. She told whoever owns the burner phone about the girl missing. The one the professor had locked up."

Laszlo growled. "That fucking imbecile was careless taking one of his own students. I cannot pull Tabitha away now to have her track that burner phone." He turned to Morax, and dread filled my lungs. "Darren, change of plans. Take a guard and bring Ms. Kingston to us. Her father wants to join The Obscuritas. Send another pair of guards to collect his wife. This will be his final test of loyalty."

Morax nodded. "Understood." His eyes snapped toward Gremory. "You. Come with us. I want you stationed outside my room. My toy does not leave, and no one goes in."

Grem nodded. "Yes, sir."

Samuel snickered. "You're so dramatic, Darren. I won't touch your little toy. I'm about to get my own."

My mind was spinning as Morax quickly tugged the leash and dragged me out of the dining room. The collar pinched, and I let them see me wince as we exited the room. Once again, our walk through the mansion was silent. Rage radiated off of Morax in waves, and he looked close to unleashing his true form.

Gremory walked silently behind us, and I didn't dare turn and look at him. Instead, I kept my head down and followed Darren like the broken thing I was supposed to be.

CHAPTER TWENTY

Morax

My entire body was itching to transform as we walked back to our room. I slipped into the guard's mind as he delivered the news of the professor's death. He had also been present in the professor's house when he abused that poor human girl. And he enjoyed it. But what nearly had me ripping his fucking head off was the fact that he was one of the men who kidnapped my girl and her father. He touched her. And seeing her chained by Darren Radnor just now got the piece of shit so aroused I slipped right into his fucking head.

I ripped open the door and ushered Michaela inside as gently as I could. As soon as the door clicked shut behind Gremory, I pushed her hair aside and tore the ugly collar from her slender neck. I pulled her close, my hands cupping her cheeks, and rested my forehead against hers. Having her close was the only thing keeping my daemon form locked down right now. I couldn't kiss her in this filthy King's body, but scenting her and touching her were enough.

She trembled in my arms, her eyes closed.

"Look at me, little lumen."

Her face turned up to mine, and I let my daemon eyes show through, reminding her who I was.

"Gremory is going to stay with you. And I am going to try desperately to save the girl."

She nodded. "What about the one the professor had?"

I shook my head. "I'm not sure where she is." I turned to Gremory. "Do you know? Were you with them at his home?"

He frowned. "Yes. I am not sorry for the professor's death. His basement was like a red room of pain. He had many photos. The last girl was not the first. He had photos of Michaela."

I snarled, and Michaela brought her hands to my face, bringing my attention back to her. "He was there when I was taken. He was hoping to have me after the Kings were done. I'm not sorry either."

"I wish he was alive so I could fucking send him back to hell myself." I was losing control, images of Michaela trapped in that sick fuck's basement invading my mind. "I'm going to disembowel that guard as well. Tony."

Michaela smirked, and I zeroed in on her mouth, needing desperately for something to stay my hand. "He's on my list of people you can put down. So, by all means."

Gremory chuckled. "Your mate has a devil side."

I prowled toward her, backing her up until her legs bumped into the bed. My eyes glowed, shining for her and only her. "Of course she does. *Though she be but little, she is fierce.*"

Michaela smiled up at me, her blue and hazel eyes holding me hostage. It was like looking into the night sky above Caligo, my home. She was mythical, otherworldly in mind, body, and soul.

"So, what happens now?" she asked, sitting back on the bed.

I crossed my arms and turned to Gremory. "Do not let a

single being near her while I am gone."

He nodded, his dark-brown eyes stoic.

"I will try to keep the Kings from finding Audrey. But I can't promise anything. If letting her escape means risking your life, I will have to bring her here and hope that we can save her some other way."

"I don't want another girl hurt because of me." Michaela shook her head, her face sullen. "That professor went home to hurt the girl he had in the basement after he left the cabin because he couldn't touch me yet. Please don't bring her here."

Pain radiated from my mate, and the growl building in my chest was loud enough to unsettle us both. She needed me, and I was failing her.

"Michaela, can you try to relax? Morax is about to unleash because he can sense your pain." Grem stepped closer to us, his hands up. A little white flag appeared, and he waved it like a jackass. "Now, Audrey may come here, but we will do everything we can to make sure she remains unharmed."

I nodded. "Yes."

Grem turned to Michaela, and she nodded as well.

"Great. Now, *Darren.* Get out of here. And watch your fucking back. Did you notice the Kings? They're agitated. Something doesn't feel right."

He wasn't wrong. I couldn't read their thoughts, but the range of emotions coming out of Samuel and Laszlo was unnerving. This had to be quick. I turned back to Michaela and knelt in front of her. She smiled at me, but it didn't meet her eyes. I took her hand and placed a kiss on her palm.

"Don't leave this room. Gremory will keep you safe."

My mate's fierce expression made it obvious she wanted to protest, but thankfully, she chose not to object. I needed to know she was safe in my absence. It would take all my focus to make sure the next few hours didn't go up in flames.

I left the room swiftly, unable to look at her again or I would fuck our plans to hell and kill them all. We were so close now. Once Seraphina arrived and The Obscuritas performed their stupid ritual, my brother would come and we could end this.

Things were not working out. I was sitting in the back of the SUV next to Audrey Kingston. She was shaking with fear. The scent was awful. The two other guards who came with me were basking in it. I almost ripped them in half for the horrible thoughts flying around in their minds when we kidnapped the girl. I chose to ride in the back with her to keep her safe from their wandering hands. Being Darren Radnor was the absolute worst, however, because he was a lecherous pig. I grabbed her by the throat when we entered her apartment. It was the only way. Darren likely would have done worse, but I just fucking could not do it.

We were almost back to the mansion, and night was falling swiftly. We had to travel by helicopter to Boston to retrieve the girl. The entire task took far too long. I sent my mind soaring after my mate. Michaela's thoughts were still closed to me, but her emotions were easy enough to read. Until the mate bond was solidified, getting a general sense of her emotions was all I could do. She was currently calm, and her relaxed state eased my own frayed nerves.

I wished I was able to help the young human coated in fear beside me, but there was nothing I could do without others noticing. I closed my eyes and focused on her recent memories. A familiar blue-haired female popped up frequently. Seraphina. She was becoming close with Michaela's sister. And she had no idea her father was currently signing up to become a cult groupie.

She did overhear her parents fighting about some of her father's new "friends," but Audrey didn't stick around to listen. Seems her parents fought frequently and she stayed away from them most of the time. Yet here she was, being dragged into her father's mess.

It was not unlike my own situation. Dragged into a war because of my father's greed and black heart. And like my fierce mate, I had two siblings equally stuck. Unfortunately, one of my brothers was pure evil and only made everything worse.

We arrived at the mansion, and I stepped out of the SUV, tugging the girl with me. I attempted to be gentle with her and simultaneously bark orders at the guards. Audrey was shaking like a leaf as I dragged her to The Study. A spike of fear from my mate had me stumbling several steps before I could collect myself. The female eyed me, confused and afraid. Something was wrong. The closer we walked to The Study, the stronger the scent of Michaela's fear became. It was palpable, invading my mind and my nose. She was not in our room.

I picked up the pace and rounded the final hallway, shoving open the doors to The Study. I noticed Laszlo Blackbyrn one second before my eyes zeroed in on Michaela. She was seated in an armchair near the fireplace, and Laszlo stood to the right of her, his hand resting casually on her shoulder. My grip on Audrey tightened, and she whimpered in pain before I realized what I was doing.

Samuel stood off to the side of the fireplace, his eyes brightening when they landed on the female.

"That was a lovely sound," he murmured. "I look forward to making you do it again."

I noted ten guards entering the room from the doors behind me. Gremory was one of them. I kept my eyes locked on Laszlo.

"What's going on here? Why do you have your hand on my toy?" Darren's voice growled out the words, laced with rage, and my daemon form ached to be unleashed.

"Now, now. She is still your toy. But we are all in this together, aren't we, Darren?" Laszlo's voice was low and slow, almost lazy. His relaxed state was more unnerving than if he were angry. I did not like this.

"We are all Kings. Equal in that, yes. And yet I have not gone after your toys. So, why did you bring mine out?" It took all of my strength to keep this form as Laszlo's grip tightened on my mate.

Michaela closed her eyes, and I felt her fear, but also her strength. She was sending me strength, willing me to remain calm. The little lumen was so much stronger than she knew.

"I want a demonstration of your power over her. You refused to let Samuel play," Laszlo continued, stepping in front of Michaela. She was wearing the collar again, and he tugged the leash, forcing her to stand. "She also seems relatively unscathed. Generally, your toys have a more haunted look about them, even after one night."

I shoved Audrey into the arms of a guard and stalked toward Laszlo. I snatched the leash out of his hand and eyed him wearily. "What kind of demonstration?"

Laszlo smirked at my outburst. His dark eyes were cold and piercing. He didn't become the leader of this deadly cult for his charm. This man was ruthless and clever.

He cocked his head to Samuel. "Samuel wanted to bring out his toys and see how you used them. But something much simpler will do. Get her on her knees and have her suck your cock."

I hesitated for half a second, and it might end up costing our lives. Laszlo noticed everything. I recovered just as fast, a lazy smirk on my face. "Gladly."

I pulled Michaela toward me and forced her to her knees. She was facing away from the others, so only I could see her face. I couldn't offer her any comfort other than sending a wave of love to her mind, letting her know how sorry I was for this.

"Take it out," I commanded, knowing Darren would do it this way.

Tears threatened to fall from her eyes, but her mouth was set in a determined line. Her fingers deftly reached up and undid my belt. She dipped her hands inside the boxers and pulled out Darren's stubby cock. Her touch was enough to make me hard, and I used that to keep up appearances of Darren's arousal. She leaned in slowly and parted her lips.

My heart broke for what I was about to do to her. I fisted a hand in her hair and forced Darren's cock down her throat. She gagged, and tears flooded her soft cheeks. I wanted to die. Gremory began whispering in my mind, begging me to let this happen. Reminding me of everything that was at stake.

I forced her to take Darren's cock deeper, and she whimpered. I looked up at Laszlo and grinned. "I like it when they cry, don't you?"

Laszlo's face remained impassive. "I thought you preferred to tie them up and beat them into compliance. This is new."

"Yeah, well, I'm adaptable." I kept the grin locked on my face. "Satisfied? Because I sure as fuck am not. I'm taking her back to my room to fuck her properly."

I shoved Michaela away and stuck the stubby cock back inside the boxers.

Gremory's voice filled my head. *You need to get the fuck out of here and take another drop of his blood. You're going to revert back soon.*

I growled, angry that he was getting into head so easily in this moment. But he was right. I grabbed Michaela's leash and pulled her toward the door, sparing a glance at the young human. She would have to be strong tonight. I couldn't do anything for her now, and that thought broke my heart. Because it was breaking my mate's heart.

How many times can I fail her before she rejects me completely?

"Have fun, Darren!" Samuel chuckled as I rushed out the door.

Laszlo said nothing, and I didn't like that one bit. Gremory was behind us, following us back to Darren's room. I could feel my daemon form coming through. My skin was starting to glow. I practically sprinted back to the room, Michaela at my side and Grem behind us. As soon as we got into the room, I dropped the leash and Michaela ran to the bathroom. Gremory whispered a few words, likely learned from his witch, and I felt the silencing magic blanket the walls. The second he finished, I roared my fury. My wings burst free, my claws extended, and I gnashed my fangs in anger. Power pulsed through my veins as I roared again, needing an outlet for my rage.

The sound of vomiting from the bathroom caught my ear, and I immediately ran to my mate. She was bent over the toilet, gagging. I gently gathered up her hair and traced my claws down her back.

"It's me, little lumen. I'm here," I whispered softly, and she shivered.

"That was awful." She mumbled the words and leaned back. I scooped her up and set her gently on the edge of the vanity.

I grabbed mouthwash from under the sink and offered her a small cup. She swished the minty liquid around in her mouth and spat it into the sink. When she looked back at me, I was relieved to see that haunted look Laszlo spoke of was nowhere to be found.

Michaela reached out and pressed her delicate hand to my cheek. I leaned into her touch, needing to feel her in my true form more than anything.

"Are you okay?" she asked.

I shook my head. "No, *mae domina*. I am not. Are you okay?"

She shook her head. "No. But it's getting better. I hated seeing you like that. Forced to do what you did."

I fell to my knees and wrapped my arms around her waist. I dropped my head in her lap, careful not to poke her with my horns. "Don't say that. Don't feel bad for me when I failed you once more. Forced his body on you. I hate this. All of this."

Michaela's soft fingers massaged my scalp, and a low purr built in my chest at the love emanating from my mate. I did not deserve her.

"Laszlo was testing you. I think he suspects something is off."

I lifted my head to stare up at her and nodded. "I think you're right."

"What do we do?" Her eyes searched mine for answers I did not have.

"Nothing right now. Your sister will be here soon. Samuel will take Audrey tonight, but his plans are minimal. She will suffer some, but not nearly as much as he plans to make her suffer later."

The sadness on my mate's face was enough to crack my heart in half. "I hate that she will suffer at all."

I nodded, standing before her and gathering her into my arms. "I do too, and I am sorry for it. They won't hurt her too badly until her father comes. And I think Laszlo plans to make that a spectacle."

"I hate him," Michaela growled, and the sound was music to my ears. I needed her strength, her fury.

I carried her into the bedroom where Gremory waited for us.

"Well, that was terrible," he quipped. I rolled my eyes, and he shrugged. "Can't say I'm surprised. These Kings are smart. Belial wouldn't be working with them if they were all complete idiots."

I sighed, taking a seat in the armchair and pulling my fearless mate into my lap. She tried to move, and I snapped my fangs at her. I needed her close right now, to feel her warmth, her strength.

"I underestimated their cleverness and I will not do so again. Guards are being dispatched now to bring Seraphina in. She will be here by tomorrow afternoon." I looked down at my mate as I spoke her sister's name.

"I haven't seen her for nearly ten years," she whispered, her voice uncertain. "I hope she's as tough as she seems to be."

Gremory chuckled. "I think the Kings have underestimated her. I'm looking forward to this, honestly."

I rolled my eyes, but internally, I prayed he was right. We needed a win. And if my brother was going to make it here, I needed Seraphina Valdis to be powerful enough to make that happen.

"If she's even half as brave as my little lumen, we have nothing to worry about." I smiled down at Michaela, and her lips turned up slightly. It was enough. For now, it was enough.

THE END
FOR NOW.

EPILOGUE

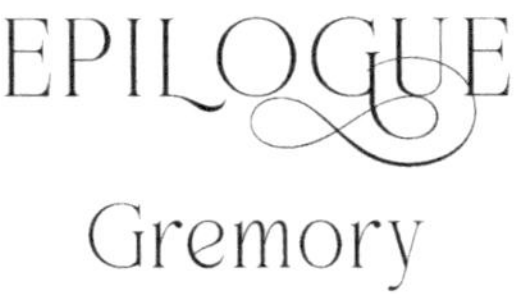

Gremory

I leaned against the wall, watching the cameras for any sign of Seraphina and the others. Being in my mortal form made my skin crawl. My spine itched where my wings usually unfurled, and I was desperate to fly. I couldn't remember the last time I took to the skies for pleasure. Well, that's not entirely true. It was with her, my pretty witch. The thought of her had my blood rushing to my dick. But it wasn't her beauty that enthralled me so. After all she has been through, my witch remained one of the most compassionate creatures I'd ever met. Her heart was pure, and I would protect it at all costs.

"Hey, you. Greg." The captain called out to me, and I resisted the urge to roll my eyes. Greg was such a dull name, but I needed to be unmemorable around the cult members.

I shoved off the wall and stood before him. He was nothing, a small man with a god complex. It was laughable, considering he had no power and I could crush his skull with my smallest finger.

"King Blackbyrn's slave has returned," he barked at me, sounding very much like the lap dog he was. "Take her to her room and make sure she chains herself up."

I nodded, hiding my revulsion. Morax told me about the

girl Laszlo Blackbyrn was enthralling. He was using power to mold her mind and force her to betray Seraphina. He also told me the girl was still in there somehow. It should be impossible for a human to withstand such control. I hadn't met her yet, so I was curious to see the little thing fighting so valiantly against daemonic power. I imagine if Laszlo had full daemonic power, her spark would've been snuffed completely. That only about a third of our power was available to him after that first ritual was likely saving her soul.

I made my way through the mansion, waiting just inside the small foyer by the servants' entrance. Two guards entered first, and when they walked past me, I caught sight of her for the first time. It took a full thirty seconds for me to recover. When her dark eyes met mine, my lungs seized and my mouth went dry. Her delicate face was filled with such infinite sadness, it nearly broke my heart. How could someone so young, so breakable, be so strong?

Tabitha dropped my gaze too soon and stared at the floor, waiting. She wore black leggings and a soft, blue sweater that dwarfed her petite frame. Her hair was cut short and choppy, and the blonde color was so light it was almost silver. I walked beside her, pressing a hand to her back to guide her gently through the manor. The other guards dispersed, not finding her a threat. We walked in silence. What could you say to someone in her position?

She had her own room on the floor below the Kings. As soon as we entered, I realized even her room was not a sanctuary. There was a small bed in the corner with a single threadbare blanket and flat pillow. The remaining space was filled with enough torture devices to mutilate a dozen people at once. It was horrifying. Even when she wasn't actively being tortured, she was surrounded by the memory of it. I reached out with my mind, attempting to sooth her, and she gasped, jumping away from me. Her body shook, and I stepped back, holding up my hands in surrender.

"I'm sorry. I didn't mean to hurt you, love."

She looked up at me with those devastating eyes.

"Usually humans can't feel it."

"I can always feel it." She whispered the words, and I frowned. The human could sense when her mind was being invaded? So every time that shitbag Blackbyrn assaulted her mind, she could feel him. But she couldn't stop him.

I took a slow step toward her, keeping my hands up in acquiescence. "I can help you."

Tabitha stepped back, shaking her head, her eyes darting to the side like a frightened rabbit. "No."

Did she know Morax was also attempting to enter her mind? Could she tell the difference between him and Blackbyrn. "Alright, love. I won't do it again. May I help you, though? I can sense you're in pain. I can heal it."

Tabitha raised her head once more. Her heart-shaped mouth was pressed into a thin line, and her eyes darted between me and the door. "I need to undress and get in my place."

The girl stepped around me and went to a closet. She stripped out of her clothes, her back to me. She wore simple white lace lingerie, barely covering her slim frame. I tried not to look, to give her some kind of privacy, but it was a struggle. Something in my blood was screaming for me to go to her. To help her. She reminded me of someone from many years ago, someone I couldn't save.

I growled. That was not going to happen again.

Tabitha slipped into a short dress designed to look like a doll's. She tucked her bright-blonde pixie cut under a wig of long, dark-brown hair then walked over to a cage in the corner of the room and opened the door.

"Wait, please." I stepped toward her, unable to watch this. "Please let me help you. I promise I won't hurt you, love."

She looked up at me again, and those eyes carried more weight than they ever should. Her gaze nearly brought me to my knees. "How? I can't escape."

I nodded. "I know. Not yet, but I can make the pain go away. Just a little. I can give you a place to retreat when things get bad."

Tabitha stared at me, her nearly lifeless eyes narrowing, assessing. I loved her instantly for her courage in this terrible situation.

She shrugged. "He will come later. Can you make me feel numb? It's all my fault, and I don't want to feel anymore. He makes me feel it."

My daemon form raged at the implications of her words. These fucking cult leaders needed to die the most excruciating deaths. I nodded and walked toward her with slow, measured steps. She was easily more than a foot shorter than me. So small, so breakable, and so fucking strong.

"Will you close your eyes?" I asked, hoping she would trust me enough to do so.

She sighed, probably thinking something awful would

happen, but then closed her eyes anyway. Such a brave little human. I let one of my claws extend and used it to cut into my pointer finger. I wrapped my fingers gently around her wrist and extended her arm then traced a symbol on her wrist, whispering a few words. The bloody mark seeped into her milky white skin and disappeared. I continued to hold her gently and brought my bloody finger to her forehead. She flinched as I traced another symbol there.

"All done."

She opened her eyes and stared at her arm where I still held her. "What happened?"

I brushed my thumb over the pulse point on her wrist. "Just a little something to help you when the pain comes. And somewhere for you to send your mind when you need a safe place. It's not enough, but it's all I can do right now."

Tabitha turned her slim face up to mine. "Thank you. You should go now."

Everything in my body screamed at me to stay and protect her, but I couldn't. Not yet. "I will come back for you, love. That's a promise."

I turned away from her before I did something horribly stupid like kidnap the girl and run away. There was too much at stake for such spontaneous heroic acts. My daemon snarled and raged for the girl. I would be back for her. It wasn't just a promise. That was a fucking oath.

ABOUT THE AUTHOR

S. D. Paine is a writer of fantasy and romance of the dark and paranormal variety. She loves a good plot twist and creating morally gray characters. She reads constantly, and cannot function without at least two cups of coffee. She lives in the Midwest with her family and a small horde of adopted dogs and a crazy cat.

www.sdpaineauthor.com

Follow the author on Facebook, Instagram and TikTok at @everafterauthor

ACKNOWLEDGEMENTS

I would like to thank my amazing editor, Andrea, and my PA, Nicole, for their constant encouragement and collaborations to make this next book come to life. Love you both! And a massive thank you to my Street Team and ARC readers. You all are the shit and I would be floating in the middle of an endless shark-infested sea without you!

The bookish community has been amazing, and I've found kick-ass friends among the readers and fellow indie authors. I am very grateful for the love you've all shown me!

And finally thank you to my friends and family. Marissa and Bri for being the best alphas/betas/arcs/listening-to-me-constantly-talk-about-the-story besties. And my core friend group, love you all for supporting me and my books!! And fam, I'm really shocked you're reading this spicy series, but love that you're here!

www.ingramcontent.com/pod-product-compliance
Lightning Source LLC
Chambersburg PA
CBHW060454300726